SHORT

Amuse ~~~**ime,**~~
and Educate

SHORT STORIES TO
Amuse, Baffle, and Educate

RON HARVEY

Short Stories to Amuse, Baffle, and Educate

Copyright © 2024 by Ron Harvey. All rights reserved.

No part of this publication may be reproduced, stored in a retrieval system or transmitted in any way by any means, electronic, mechanical, photocopy, recording or otherwise without the prior permission of the author except as provided by USA copyright law.

The opinions expressed by the author are not necessarily those of URLink Print and Media.

1603 Capitol Ave., Suite 310 Cheyenne, Wyoming USA 82001
1-888-980-6523 | admin@urlinkpublishing.com

URLink Print and Media is committed to excellence in the publishing industry.

Book design copyright © 2024 by URLink Print and Media. All rights reserved.

Published in the United States of America
Library of Congress Control Number: 2024922296
ISBN 978-1-68486-960-2 (Paperback)
ISBN 978-1-68486-964-0 (Digital)
08.10.24

A Tale of A Fish Tale or A Fish Story

The earliest recorded sightings of fish occurred in Finland by Ian "The Huckster" Finn. Obviously this is why fish fins are called fins and Finlanders are called Finns. The reason Finland is so named is that finicky Finnish fishermen were landing these finned denizens of the deep all over the land. There were Finns and fins in fens and fjords everywhere. Don't fence me fin, Norway am I Finnish yet. How Sweden it is. Don't give up yet, you could get hooked on this story or is that de-baitable?

Fish could not have been named before the first one was caught. Who named the first fish. I only wish we knew Who's last name and why he decided to name them "fish." Probably it had something to do with the Finnish pronunciation of "wish" as in "Vow, luke at a deese ting Sven! I <u>fish</u> I kanew vaht it vahs." He didn't do it on porpoise I'm sure.

Once the early Finns discovered that fish were edible, many methods were devised to capture them - not the Finns, the fish. One of the first methods was to use tall slender bamboo cane "poles" (from Poleland, obviously). These early fishermen and fisherwomen would wade into the water with the canes and bam them loudly in the water while yelling, BOO! This would cause the fish to be frightened into convulsive fits of unswimmable flotation and become easily caught. This is also how bamboo was named.

The most successful method was the gill net designed by an old Finlander named Olaf "Gil" Olafson. Smaller fish were able to swim through the meshed opening but the larger fish would get their heads stuck and found themselves in quite a mesh. Since fish don't swim very well in reverse, they couldn't back out. The net effect was that they were stuck. This net was named the gill net in honor of "Gil" Olafson as were the gills of fish since that was the portion of their anatomy that caused them to become trapped (actually it was the opercular flap, but the Finns kept that a secret until the early 1800's). The second "l" in gill was added just for the "L" of it. Some people thought Gil was in seine, but he was knot. Soon after Gil's success, netmakers flourished. They all went dutch, bought netmaking supplies, and moved to another part of the country. The land inhabited by these netmakers became known as the Netterlands.

The musical scales were also discovered by musicaly inclined frenetic Finnish fishermen. After the first Finnish fish fry on Friday (originally called Fryday because of this fish frying tradition) a few fickle Finns suggested that for the next fish fry perhaps removing the scales (how they came to be called scales will be described shortly) would improve the fish's palatability somewhat.

Fish

It was during this scale removal process they noticed that the scales made musical sounds as they whirred through the air. The larger scales made the low, or bass (not to be confused with the Lower Bass, which is a type of fish) sounds and the smaller scales made the higher pitched whirring sounds. Soon, they began arranging the dried scales on keyboards (made from the Key tree) in an ascending order of pitch. Pitch was used to glue the scales to the keyboard and the person gluing them would yell, "bring me some more pitch!! The musical scales could be played by plucking them with the fingernails. At first, someone suggested the scales "be flat" on the board but "a sharp" person placed them upright for easier plucking. The music caused people to scale walls. This is why scales are named scales.

The Story of Al Ergy

Ron Harvey
October, 2002

Al Ergy should have been a track star. He always had runny eyes and a runny nose. No matter what you had to say, he always agreed that it was something to sneeze at. His favorite T-shirt had his favorite word on the front (Pollen) and his favorite number (8) on the back. Al had a very good personality in spite of all of his adverse reactions. People often called him the charismatic asthmatic. It is a good thing he didn't excel in math or they would have called him the charismatic asthmatic mathmatic.

Al could have chosen another avocation other than being an official Vidalia Onion tester. He could have easily chosen to be a phlegm flam artist. It was a choice that boogered him for the rest of his life. Lord nose.... He once considered becoming a mortician because he was always coughin'. And there was the time he was going to go into business with his brother Roofus the roofer, but he was afraid he might have to get the shingles. For a brief time he even considered becoming a taxi driver but was repulsed at the thought of people calling him a hacking hack. I surmise that this was the primary reason for his leaving Hackensack, New Jersey. Can you imagine what people might have said when he went to bed? Well, there goes the hacking hack from Hackensack hacking in the sack. I'm sure that would have become a hackneyed expression after a while.

Can you guess what Al Ergy's favorite sport was? Why it was sniffle ball, of course. Although occasionally, he liked to play chest. The only problem he had playing chest was when he checked his mate, she was up to some hanky-panky. Obviously, she had no choice because Al was always in need of a hanky. She was particular in the way she handed it to him - always dangling from her pinky finger. He affectionately called it her hanky-panky pinky.

Al once considered joining the military- the Air Force in particular- because when he sneezed he had an abundance of air force. Instead, he joined the Nasal Reserves. He thought about joining the Marines but didn't want to be called a jar-head' although he wistfully thought that maybe a good jar to the head would relieve some of his congestion.

Al liked to visit his relatives. There was his cousin Septum, who was a deviate. His other cousin Ek Zema, who was always scratching around for something and just itching to see him. Ek always welcomed Al with a hearty, 'Wheeze sho glad to see you, Al". His cousin Ivy was another favorite, but she was always making rash decisions. Ivy was always poised on the verge of making a breakthrough, but never could scratch the surface. His favorite relatives were his auntie Histamine and uncle Al Egra. They were a sure cure for his miseries.

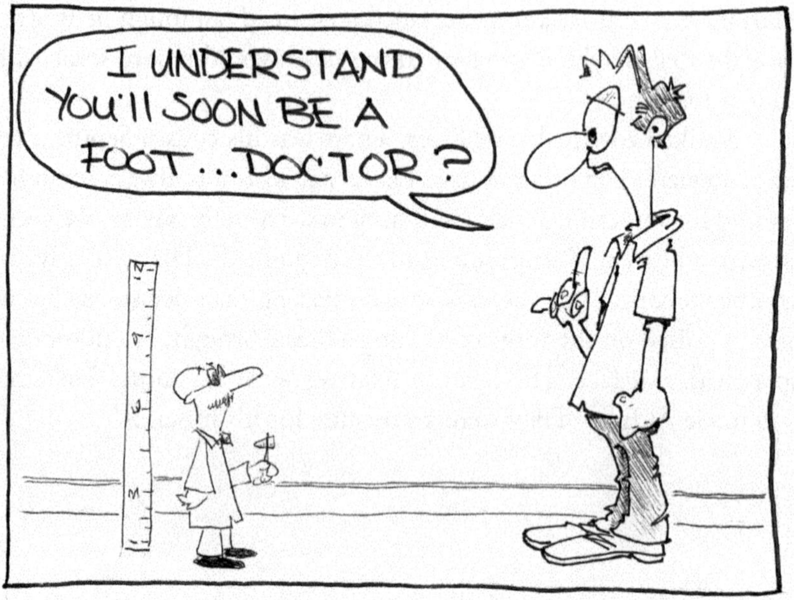
I UNDERSTAND YOU'll SOON BE A FOOT...DOCTOR?

A Case of a Sole Sole and Sole Cell in a Cell in Seoul
Better it be known as the "Tale of a Fish Tail in Jail."

Copyright 8 November 29, 1995

This is the story of a dissenting amoeba named Amelia who longed to go to Korea and seek a second career as an agent of Amoebic Dysentery. All her life she just piddled in puddles with her paramecium pals. Then one day she was plucked from her puddle of paramecium pals on the sole of a sandy sandel worn by a hapless beachcomber bum. Little did Amelia the amoeba know that the hapless beachcombing bum was headed to the fish market. There was a whale of a sole sale that day. It was the blue light special of fish sales. Upon seeing all of those flipping fish, she thought to herself, "What a bunch of carp." She quietly slipped from the sandy sandel sole and floundered about a bit. Suddenly, a flounder flipped onto the floor. Then a slippery sole on sale sailed from an unstable table and just filleted there. This was the opportune moment to carpe diem, carp or not. Onto the unsold sole tail she sailed. With a few phlegmatic flips of its tail, the sole flopped to the edge of the dock and fell to the water below. Together they sailed the sea to see Seoul's seashore. Amelia the amoeba had arrived in Seoul sailing on the tail of an unsold sole and left home without telling a soul about the sole or Seoul.

Suddenly, she felt the net effect of a Korean fishing fleet.

She and the sole were hauled aboard and packed on ice. It was a chilling experience. This was the only sole with a lone amoeba on its tail that the fisherman caught all day which made it the sole sole with a sole cell.

Later, the unsold sole sole was sold to the Seoul constable.

The sole pleaded with the constable to let him go, but it was a one sided argument (it had to be since the sole is first cousin to the flounder).

As the constable was preparing to cook the sole that evening, the sole turned the tables on him. Amelia tickled the sole's tail and he began flipping. First, he knocked over the salt shaker. Then he turned over the bowl of batter. The constable became very angry and had them both arrested for a salt and batter. Poor Amelia and the sole ended up in jail which makes this a tall tale of sole tail and a sole cell in a cell in Seoul.

The HAT looks good on you, but I think you need another COLOR.

A Fine Arrangement

Copyright 7 1993 by Ron Harvey

The human body is a fine arrangement of form and functionality. But, have you ever wondered what it might be like if our parts were slightly rearranged and/or modified? What good are armpits? Would we be better off without them? What if our arms were located on our hips, and we had four armpits? For starters, our deodorant expenses would double and if we had underarm perspiration problems, we wouldn't know whether to raise our arm or lower it. Putting on shoes and socks might be a little easier, but combing our hair could be a reach. Nose pickers might be a little put out by this arrangement, and we could no longer wipe our noses on our shirtsleeve. Scratching our backs wouldn't be any easier unless one arm was reversed. If that were the case there would be no more, "you scratch my back, I'll scratch yours". Doing cartwheels would be more difficult, but would push-ups? I guess that would depend upon whether we were top heavy or bottom heavy. Either way, we would make a good seesaw for the kids.

Chiropractors would become obsolete since we wouldn't need to bend or stoop to pull weeds, lift heavy objects, or tie our shoes.

Holding hands (or feet) under the table would be less conspicuous. Instead of just playing "footsies", we could also play "handsies" or "handsies and footsies." Dropped table utensils would be much easier to retrieve, wipe semi clean, and place back on the table unnoticed. They might even be easier to catch before they hit the floor.

Think of the changes that would have to be made in the clothing industry: Pants pockets would need to be about cuff high or else we couldn't easily get to our pocket change. Certainly no one else could get their hands in our pockets because they would always be.....a foot away. Men could discreetly scratch their feet instead.

Shirtsleeves could be eliminated and we would have pantsleeves instead. They could no longer be called a "pair" of pants. They would have to be referred to as "a quadruple" of pants. Levi 501's would have to be renamed Levi 1002's. Designer suspenders could either be eliminated or made much shorter.

Body language would have to be reinterpreted. Would our hands on our knees instead of our hips still be a sign of frustration or something entirely different? What about folding the arms across the groin instead of the chest? Would that signal disinterest or merely indicate that we're doing something we can no longer do because our pockets are too low?

TWO MORE PEOPLE GOT FIRED TODAY.
EASTMAN CHEMICALS
YIKES!
OH NO!

Apparently So

Copyright © October, 1998
Revised June, 2000
K. R. Harvey

A pair of pears was peering over a pair of piers, or at least it apparently appeared. This pair of pears belonged to a gentleman whose name perchance happened to be Bart. Bart had owned this particular pair of pears for a pair of years, so he was quite content to let them peer at their leisure – or at piers. Since Bart let them do this; they became known as Bartlett pears. This pair of peering pears soon became discontented with merely peering at piers and began appearing at windows and peering at Bart's peers. This was clearly a case of Bart's pears peering at Bart's peers. Bart's peers were understandably upset over Bart's pair of peering pairs and began lodging complaints against Bart. Shortly, Bart had so many complaints lodged against him, that he had to call the rescue squad to have them dislodged. Bart appealed to the pears to stop their voyeuristic peering, but it was to no avail. It soon became "impearative" that Bart devise a plan to impair the pears peers lest the peering pears invite their peers to join them in their peering pairings. If this came to be, Bart would surely have so many complaints lodged against him that he would be unable to move. Desperate for a solution, he mixed water and whiskey. He then recalled and reiterated his pleas: "please, please, please, I'm pleading, cease peering at my peers." His please, please, please, pleas fell upon deaf pears. Suddenly, Bart remembered that his initial pleas were to no avail, which inspired an available plan to which he availed himself.

He would toss a veil over the pair of peering pears the next time they crossed the vale for one of their daring peering escapades. He had to be careful not to unveil his veil plan in the vale for fear that the pair of peering pears pummel him. There's nothing worse than being pummeled by a pair of peering pears. As an added precaution, Bart decided to take along his trusty paring knife in the event he needed to pare the pair of peer peering pears.

The trap was set. Bart hid in the vale and awaited the unsuspecting pair of peering pears. As soon as they tumbled across the vale (pears can't walk you know), Bart tossed the veil over them. One of the pears screamed, "This is a veiled threat, tumble for your life!" It was no use. The pair of peering pears was veiled in the vale. Bart appeared and appeared angrily as he approached the hapless pair of peering pears with his paring knife. "I'm appealing to you one last time to stop your peering, he belched, or I shall begin a-peeling you both with this paring knife and that is nor appealing." It just so happened that the pair of peering pears was addicted to peering and would not give in to Bart's please, please, please, pleas. Bart had no choice but to draw his paring knife and commence peeling the wayward pair of pears. The pear's screams pealed across the vale as their peels were pared. Bart apologized to the pair of peering pears for the paring: " Please forgive me for the paring, pear pair. I'm merely a pear bearer bearing a bare paring knife in order to bare peering pears, so please don't bear any hard peelings towards me."

I can't bear it any longer, as I'm sure you can't either, so this is the end of this unpearable story.

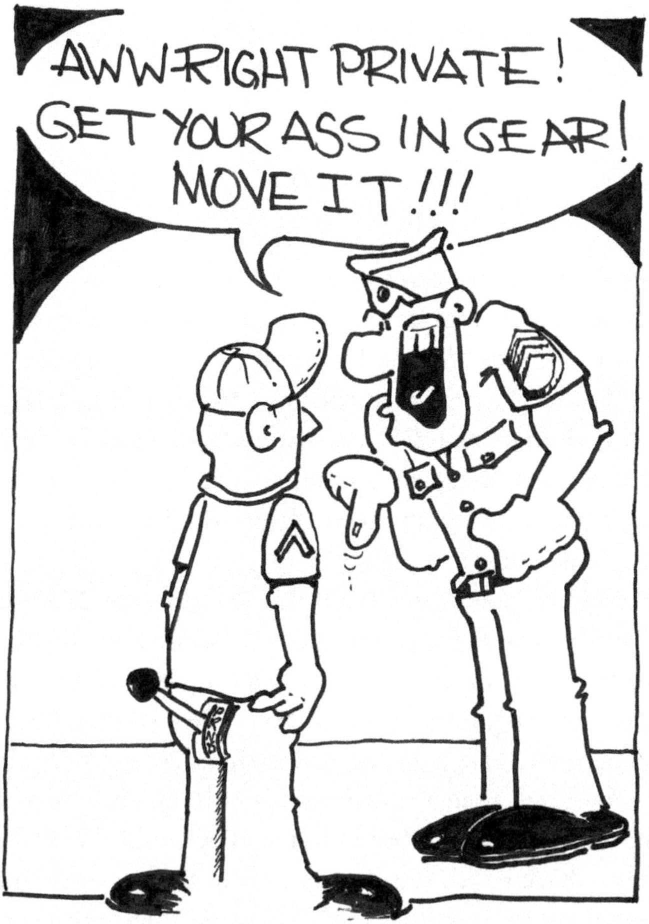
AWW-RIGHT PRIVATE! GET YOUR ASS IN GEAR! MOVE IT!!!

The First Baseball Game

by
Ron Harvey
10/26/93

The inspiration for this came as I watched game four of the World Series. It was the bottom of the sixth and the Phillie's were leading the Toronto Blue Jays 13 to 9. With this sort of scoring, it should be renamed the Whirl Series what with the players whirling around the bases and whirling around in the batters box. Heck, even the fans were whirling handkerchiefs around in the bleachers. I wonder if anyone ever got bleached up there? If they did, I guess it would be an enwhitening experience.

Baseball began after the domestication of the guinea fowl. Back in the days of feudal fiefdom, the peasants became bored after serfing in the amber waves of grain all day. After a particularly boring day, they noticed several guinea fowl in a nearby field chasing little wriggly worms. This particular field was later named Wriggly Worm Field. Since the peasants used the worms for fishing, they proceeded to throw the guinea fowl out, but as fast as they could throw them out, the fowl flew back in. To solve this problem, the peasants plucked all of the feathers from the guinea fowl. The guineas were first called bald fowls and later nicknamed "baldies". This still didn't keep the fowl out, because as soon as the peasants turned their backs, the baldies would roll back onto Wriggly field. The peasants had to find another solution.

Roaming the kingdom was a lion with a very deep roar. The lion was captured and trained to walk the edges of Wriggly Worm Field while roaring with his deep voice. The lion soon became known as the bass lion. This strategy worked for a while, but the bald fowl were determined to play on Wriggly Worm field. They appealed throughout the empire complaining that they weren't being treated as fair balds. The only answer they received was, "Um…um..um". The empire was soon being called the Um-pire by the bald fowls. The peasants had had enough so they loaded the recalcitrant fowl onto a coach and brought them back to Wriggly Worm Field. This is also how the term "coach", as applied to team managers, was derived.

The pitchers mound is so called because the peasant began pitching fits after pitching their tents on a mound in the middle of Wriggly Worm field. This is also where they kept pitchers of water to quench their thirst after chasing bald fowls or "baldies on Wriggly field. Finally the solution came to them as to how they could rid Wriggly Worm field of the bald fowls. As the bald fowl were caught, they were struck out by a person called the "designated hitter". The peasants then basted them with a sauce (at this time the baldies were called basted baldies - hence the term baseball) and tossed them to a "catcher who then tossed them into a box of batter (later named the batterer's box after the peasant who made the box and prepared the batter in which to cook the basted baldies). All of the other peasants would bring plates from home and stand by the batterer's box to be served. This area around the batterer's box was came to be called "home plate". I guess first, second and third base were named after the number of times a baldie had to be basted before finally being battered. From here, it's easy to see how the present form of baseball evolved from this early sport.

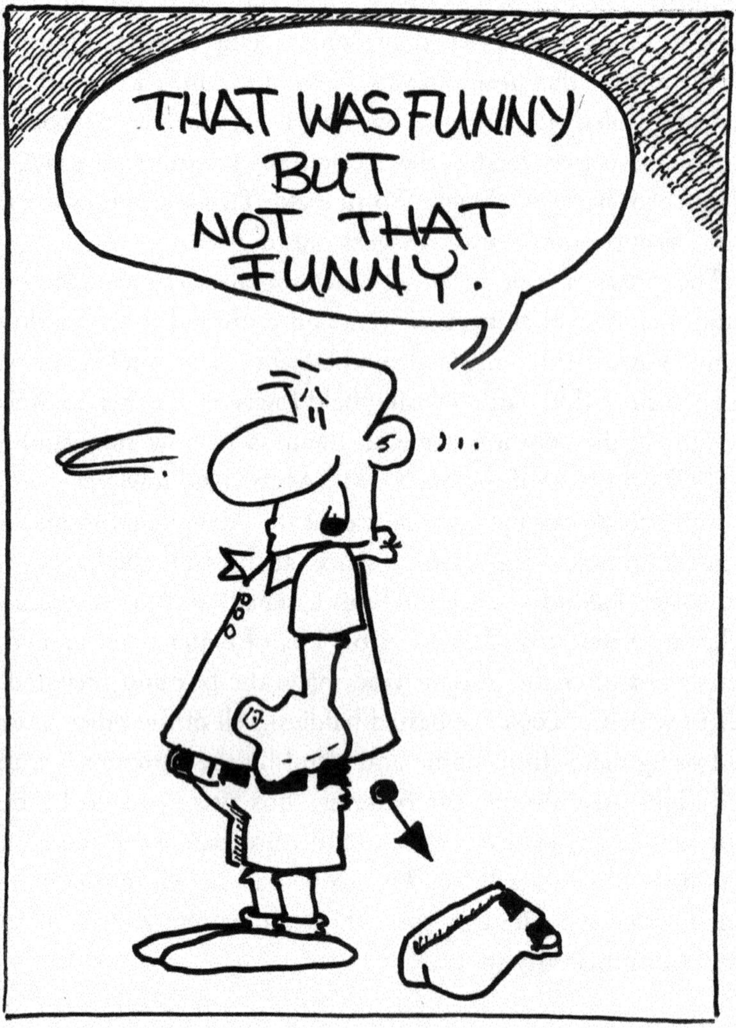
THAT WAS FUNNY BUT NOT THAT FUNNY.

The Booty and The Bee-ist

Copyright 8 1993 by Ron Harvey

Once upon a time, in the small town of Willowbee, there lived a keeper of bees. The local folk called him a bee-ist because he knew all there was to know about bees. He knew bees inside and out, but mostly out. Getting to know them inside took a lot of guts, which the bees didn't particularly appreciate since it was their guts. He bee-gan his hobby of bee keeping bee-fore the songs "I just Gotta Bee Me" and "Let it Bee" (by the Bee-tles) became popular. After his first encounter with bees, he said it gave him a swarm feeling all over and he felt swell.

The bees loved him and produced copious quantities of honey that he sold to honey lovers all over. Why they liked honey all over is bee-yond me. Honey lovers traveled from Afar, which was a small town not far from Willowbee, to taste of his wares - which he sold in addition to honey. So prized was the bee-ist's honey, that honey aficionados paid Handsomely (his real name) for his nectar. The means by which they paid was to hand craft small booties for the bees to wear that enhanced their pollen collecting ability (the bee's, not the people from Afar). For each small jar of honey, the people from Afar would pay Handsomely handsomely and trade three pairs (enough for one bee) of small booties - size 6-B in bee sizes. The bees were very pleased because they didn't have to work as hard. It was neat because the queen bee had high heeled booties, the worker bees had steel toed booties, and the drones and upper management bees had booties with little tassels. Of course their favorites were the wing tip booties.

In due time, the bee-ist decided he had to diversify to make more honey money. He instructed the bees to collect pollen from persimmon trees. The result was bittersweet. He pushed them harder to produce more. The bees bee-gan to protest. The easiest way for them to do this was to have an uprising. The bee-ist would have none of this, so he threatened them with a bee-bee gun. The bees would have none of that, so they set up a sting operation. The bee-ist got wind of the sting operation and became nervous and contracted a case of the hives. This didn't stop the bees. The next time they saw the bee-ist, they lit upon him and began kicking him in his eyes with their bee booties.

This was definitely a case of bootie being in the eyes of the bee holder.

I'M STARVED!
OH BOY AT LAST ME TOO!
THIS TIME YOU TAKE THE ONE ON THE LEFT!
McSnakes

This Is For The Birds

Copyright © 1993 by Ron Harvey

The evolution of the avian species must have truly been a remarkable thing. I imagine it took several million years for the first bird to develop and meet all the specifications of a fully qualified flyer.

Fossil records show that the first birds supposedly arose from the archosaurs, which produced the flying reptiles and the flying leap. As specialized as the bird wing is, it had to be the next to last bird part to develop. The first bird had only one wing and flew in circles. Depending on whether it was a left wing or right wing, the bird either flew clockwise or counter-clockwise. We still have right wingers and left wingers today that fly in circles.

After birds got around to growing two wings, they could only fly straight up or straight down since they had not developed the tail feathers yet. As a matter of fact, the dove (originally pronounced as the past tense of dive) was so named because it was one of the first birds to attempt flying without tail feathers and immediately dove back to earth. It is my theory that tail feathers later developed due to this straight up and straight down aerial maneuver. As the bird rose vertically, the blood rushed to the posterior region of the bird's body thus stimulating tail feather growth. The tail was a stabilizing factor and greatly enhanced the bird's flight patterns. It has always puzzled me as to why birds grew a tail instead of another wing. I guess if they had, we would have another species known as the "helibirds" because their flight would resemble that of a helicopter.

Although the logic behind the naming of the dove is indisputable, the naming of other bird's is mystifying. For example: how did the pigeon get it's name? I can only surmise that the pigeon is a descendant of flying pigs and it took eons for them to become un-pig-like. It was the combining of "pigs" and "eons" that this bird was so named. It was during this evolutionary phase of the pigeon that cave men were heard saying, "Look! Up in the sty! It's a bird, it's a pig! No, it's a pig-eon!

What about the Nuthatch? Do they really hatch nuts? Was the Robin caught stealing? Was the Duck trying to avoid being hit? Surely the Killdeer can't kill deer. Is the Bluebird really sad?

Sparrows were named by the Indians. Since the sparrow was such a small and difficult target, many arrows were often required to bag a daily limit. The plains Indians who hunted them resorted to carrying spare arrows for this reason. It was the contraction of "spare" and "arrow" that led to this little bird's name.

I won't speculate as to the naming of the Tufted Titmouse or the Woodpecker.

Jr. provided a stool sample to his doctor as requested.
LAB
Flu shots now
1%

To Da' Boss

Today we celebrate Bosses Day

For tis him we honor and obey
He has the knowledge and darn well knows
Who amongst has the brownest nosw

Lest this turn out to be a morbid wake
Our ISO lusters brought you chocolate cake
Because you are the best in our eyes
We've also brung you chocolate pies

Roses are red and violets are blue
Chocolate is brown and our noses are too
So from the Harem and the rest of us
Eat brownies til you but

Claud's Golfing Poem

Iff'n the tee times of two oh two
Be lookin' good for good ole you
That'll surely suit good ole me
To see you at that time on the tee

We'll whack that little round ball
Watch it rise and oft too quickly fall
Golf with you can be fun and nice
Especially when you curse your slice

Ron Harvey

The gentle "whoosh whoosh whoosh whoosh"
Of a tossed club flying towards a myrtle boosh
Is usually a dead give-away and tell tale sign
That your shot wasn't exactly on line

When a putt rims the cup but doesn't fall
I'm alert for a flying putter and reprimanded ball
We'll laugh as we leave the green
Lamenting, "ain't that the dangdest thing you done ever seen?"

The Tale of Mr. Cliff Hanger

Ron Harvey
November 6, 2003

Cliff Hanger was a mountain of a man, but only in the sense that he was as tall as a mountain. He stood about 7' 2" and weighed only 123 pounds. People called him a "foothill" because he was only a foot shy of being as tall as the highest hill in town. Besides that, he didn't have a car and was always afoot. Such a strange name too. He was named after his German grandfather Kliffen Hankerstein

Cliff loved tinkering and almost became a tinker but didn't give a tinker's damn about household utensils. However, his love of tinkering led him into other avocations. He even had an aviation avocation, which led him to the invention of the hang glider. Originally it was called a Hanger Glider but the name was changed to Hang Glider after he finally got the hang of jumping from cliffs with it. People would stand in Awe (the small town where Cliff lived) and watch as Cliff stood on the cliff and prepared to take his first flight. It was truly a real cliffhanger.

Cliff and his family were very close. As a matter of fact, people called them a bunch of close hangers. Cilff was so touched (many people thought he was a little touched) by this, he was inspired to invent the clothes hanger as well as the airplane hangar. Needless to say, Cliff wasn't one to just hang around so he hung wallpaper in Stead (a small town near Awe). This is actually where the term "hangnail" originated. Cliff wasn't very adept at hanging wallpaper, so he would nail it in place. He hit his thumbs so often with the hammer that they were always sore. People couldn't believe he was so inept. They actually drew thumbnail sketches of him.

    Cliff wasn't without his flaws. I'm not sure exactly what a flaw is, but I'm told he kept several in his shirt pocket as well as his personality. He eventually became so depressed that he hung himself in his closet. It was a very tall closet.

Clothes Friends and Close Calls

by
Ron Harvey 6/12/1993

Once, a Pun of Thyme, and a man named Noah, moved from the tiny town of Thyme just in time. You see, The Ewe Sea was near Bye, which is another town a short time from Thyme. Justin, The Nick of Thyme, was a clothes friend of Noah before everyone knew Noah as Noah. Through a Quirk of Fate (there were many quirks in the town of Fate, as fate would have it), Noah's name was changed from NaOH because of a caustic reaction. Needleless to say (there were no needles in Volved, which just happens to be the town where this incident occurred) there were many caustic remarks to B. Herd. Mr B. Herd was to blame, but let's leave it be. Some things were not mint to B. Herd, but perhaps some other flavor instead.

Back to Justin, the Nick of Thyme (I have no earthly idea what a Nick was or what sort of occupation it involved in Volved). Justin was always flipping nickels with his knuckles. One day, a not so sharpshooter of arrows of the crossbow crossed Beaux (the river between Bye and Thyme) and saw Justin knuckle flipping nickels. Well, it just so happens that the not so sharp sharpshooter was amiss. A miss who couldn't resist taking a shot at one of the flipping nickels.

Smiling as she drew the bow, she put away the pencil and paper, and let the arrow fly (an Arrow Fly is a small fly lost in Thyme). I'm sure you have heard that a miss is as good as a smile. In this (brief) case, the smile exerted a slight excess of pressure on her right eye muscles and caused her to be a bit off target. As to who bit it off, I don't know.

By now (actually bye later, for the story's not quite finished) you might have guessed, the arrow nicked the nickel and the nickel nicked the Nick (Justin), Hence, he became the Nick of Thyme. It was a close call, after all, because he had to call the clothing store for more clothes. "Help, he said. I've just had an arrow escape and I must say, I need some new clothes." Who Do You Think worked at the clothing store, but was out ill that day, so Noah worked for him in Stead (the town in which the clothing store was located). Justin was relieved (at this point an underwear statement) to speak with Noah. It was often said (although not too often, since repeating things was repetitious and difficult in this particular instance) that "no nose knows clothes like Noah's nose". In this case, Noah's nose knew Justin needed new clothes. This is why Justin and Noah were clothes friends. Think I'll close on that note.

Cranial Flatulence

By
Ron Harvey

They always seem to come at the most inopportune moments and are often referred to as "brain pharts". I prefer cranial flatulence because it just sounds nicer and can be "passed" off as a medical condition. Everyone has them, but they increase in frequency and duration as we get older, totally mimicking intestinal gas but without the odor. If you haven't experienced cranial flatulence yet, don't get too comfortable-it will come. I've heard it called senior moments which is totally incorrectum. Yes, this is actually a word, which, by the way, is defined in Webster's dictionary as, the incorrect method of expelling gas, Senior moments occur when you drink too much prune juice. Cranial flatulence is quite possibly the result of not drinking enough prune juice. I believe herein lies the cause. If gas is not properly expelled (loudly and with as much force as is safely allowed), it builds in the body and eventually rises to one's head thereby interrupting neuronal activity and causing disruptions in the thought and reactivity process.

Cranial flatulence is quite the dilemma and can be very embarrassing if not handled with proper aplomb. It is potentially more embarrassing when accompanied with cranial crepitations. Please allow me to give an analogy. Cranial flatulence is analogous to the infamous Silent but Deadly fart. It occurs without much ado, unless, of course, you happen to be in a crowded elevator. In this situation, you can easily place the blame on someone else by appearing to be totally offended and complaining loudly. With brain pharts, there is no placing blame. You must accept responsibility simply because it will be obvious.

Cranial flatulence with crepitations is always accompanied by some sort of noisy utterance or mumbling. Crepitations are totally involuntary reactions. You just automatically feel that you have to blurt out some sort of explanation as to your stupidity. How you handle yourself in these situations says a lot about your character. It is best not to shout out loudly such phrases as: "What the hell was I thinking!" "Did you see what I just did ?" or, "Can you believe that?" This just draws more attention to your mistake.

When experiencing cranial flatulence with crepitations, it is best to be as discrete as possible. Look for outside causes or distractions to explain your momentary lapses in memory or judgement. A good example is the ploy often used by experienced flatulators: "Wow. There sure are a lot of those barking spiders out today!" or, "Did someone just step on a duck? Don't use these when you have a brain phart or someone will think you actually committed an flatuary indiscretion. Try saying something like, "I shouldnt have taken my wife's medication by mistake this morning" or, "I must have laced my shoes too tightly today," (check to make sure you aren't wearing loafers before using this one).

Controlling crepitations and limiting the incidence rate of cranial flatulence can be challenging. I hope this will be of some guidance in helping you cope with your next (or first) episode of cranial flatulence.

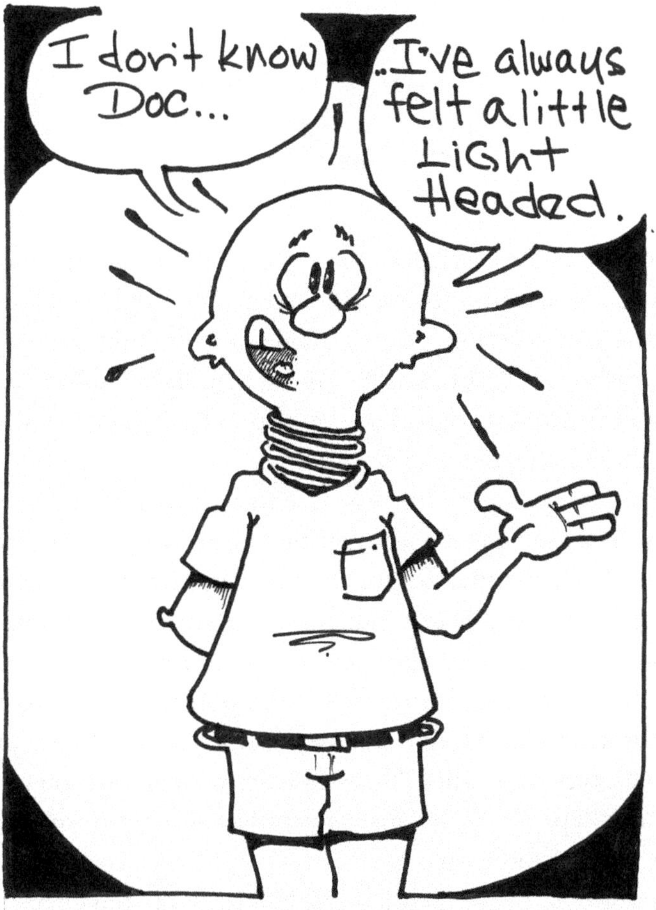
I don't know Doc...
...I've always felt a little Light Headed.

Etymology of Fly

Copyright © 10/04/91
by
Ron Harvey

As I pondered the enigmatic poser presented to me this morning as related to the ubiquitous, omnipresesent (although its ubiquity was mitigated to a tolerable extent, thanks to a friendly fungi-probably polyhedrosis) order of diptera (more familiarly known as musca domesticus), I was intrigued by the plethora of possibilities as to how the fly came to be called a fly.

Your reasoning of "why wasn't a bird called a fly" is a good point to consider except for the fact that birds were originally called "flaps" because of the manner in which they conducted themselves while airborne. Those unable to conduct themselves in an airborne manner and suddenly discovered themselves in a groundborne situation were promptly called "flops" since this is the past tense of flap. Those of the avian species who found themselves stuck in the chimneys of early piltdown caves were called "flews". Hence the conjugation of the verb flew- flew, flap, flip, flop (this conjugation also led to the naming of certain types of footwear).

According to dipterian hieroglyphics and drawings smuggled from the caves of Lascaux, these pteryginous insects were first called "ylfs" by pleistocenic, wooly mammoth hide wearing Cro-Magnon men (this also leads to the reason filet-mignon is so named, but I shan't go into that now). Women were allowed to wear only the skin of rabbits. This fashionable attire was called, "hide hare". This is also the reason rabbits came to be called hares and hides are called hides. Because their furs (this is another entire treatise, " Etymology of Fur") actually "hided" hair (they weren't aware of past tenses yet). I can't account for this early difference in the spelling of hair and hare, but that's neither hear nor there. Here, here.

"Ylfs" were so called because of the sounds Cro-Magnon man made while attempting to swat these pestiferous, coprophagous and proliferatively copulative pests from their wooly mammoth hides. The reason the ylfs were so attracted to Cro-Magnon man was the wooly mammoth hides--most of the time they still contained significant portions of the hapless mammoth itself.

Eventually, the swatting of ylfs came to be major contests among nomadic tribes. The groups would get together over a meal of hot and spicey pterodactyl wings and sit around the fire "popping ylfs" with pterodactyl drumsticks. The winner was the one who could pop the greatest number of ylfs. The loser was the one with the most ylf viscera on his wooly mammoth suit. The word "viscosity" had its origins from this sport also. The poor loser had so many ylf viscera on his suit, it became difficult for him to move about and his cohorts said that he was suffering from high "viscerosity" (hence the derivation of the word viscosity).. Believe it or not the baseball term "pop fly" originated from this very same sport as the term "ylf" was eventually bastardized by the Bastillian hordes invading (and later interpreting) this part of the world. The interpreters thought they had magnifying glasses to read the records of theses ylf popping tribes, but they were actually mirrors so the term "ylf pop" actually came out "pop fly". This is why flys are called flys.

Willy was always PUTTING a PLUG in for his SPONSORS.
Will this one do?

The Joys of Air Travel

Copyright © 1993 by Ron Harvey

Today, my gate was changed three times - as well as my gait. Fortunately, I arrived at the Atlanta terminal with a little time to spare. I checked the departure monitors for my flight. Gate B31. No problem. I've learned to remove everything from my pockets before going through the metal detectors; keys, money clip, loose change, ammo clips, bayonets, hand grenades, bazooka, and howitzers. Some people never learn. They still try to get past security with loose change.

Down the escalator to the subway. Today, there was one of life's rejects with a four by ten foot sign extolling the virtues of Romans 10:13 by the entrance to the train. Not that I'm against the virtues of Romans 10:13, but I'm sure that most travelers don't want to take the time to be "saved " at the doors of a subway while trying to make their flight on time. That's another thing that torques my jaws. These idiots that stand directly in front of the train while people are trying to get off. Just once I'd like to see about ten of them get knocked on their duffs by an exiting Green Bay Packer.

I arrive at my gate, drop my bag, make a quick phone call to the office, and recheck my gate and departure time. Departure time is okay, but the gate is no longer B31. It's been changed to B36. These things happen. I get to gate B36 and check in with the agent. He took my ticket and said he'd call me when seating was available (I was flying standby). I took a seat, read the Miami Herald, the Washington Post, and the flight destination and departure time on the digital display over the gate's ticket counter. It read:...FLIGHT 987....... BATON

ROUGE....DEPARTING..... 11:58. My flight was:....FLIGHT 726....CHARLESTON, SC.....DEPARTING 11:51.......WHAT THE H...!! Another gate change. Now it's B5. That'll teach me to read newspapers when the airlines decide to play musical gates. For those of you who have never been in the Atlanta airport, gate B36 is the last gate at the far end of the B concourse. B5 is about three and a half miles down on the opposite end.

Now the fun part. First they "Preboard" the plane. How do they do that? Do they load lumber before they begin loading people? This is like saying: " passengers pre-get on the plane." Either people board or they don't. Some passengers need to be pre-boarded...preferably with a two by four.

Why is it that I always get the seat next to a 372 pounder with dandruff, a bad cough, a hair brush, and no handkerchief? It's wouldn't be so bad if it were on the three seat side of the aircraft, but this phenomena always occurs on the two seat side. I could be on a flight with a full years supply of Ed McMahon's Starsearch spokesmodels and be assigned the seat next to Ed. To add insult to Flying injury, the person in front of me is a recliner. The Gospel truth. On the flight to Atlanta, there was only one person on the plane with his seat reclined. You guessed it. More Gospel truth. On the flight back to Charleston, there were only two "recliners". One who's seat back held my "tray table" and the other was across the aisle. If there were a flock of "recliners" on a flight, I'd be in the seat behind them.

Screaming kids. I think parents with screaming, unruly, crying kids check with the airlines to see if I'm on a particular flight. Then they book it. Once, I had the luxury of having three seats to myself on a flight to New York. There was a young mother with an "adamantly opposed to flying" child about four rows behind me. About 38 seconds after becoming airborne, she brings this screaming kid up to where I am sitting and puts her in the two empty seats with me....and goes back to her seat. It was a most enjoyable flight. As if having to go to New York City isn't bad enough.

I like it when the flight attendants announce: "Please have all cups and glasses ready so we may collect them as we pass through the aisles." This I have to see. Perhaps David Copperfield could pass through an aisle at 35,000 feet, but not your average flight attendant. I've often wondered about the dangers a flying plastic cup might pose during a plane crash. Does it make sense that we aren't allowed to have an empty plastic cup while taxiing at 7 miles per hour but it's okay while flying at 535 miles per hour?

"Welcome to Charleston, the terminating point for our flight." May I please "pre-deplane" before that happens?

Sarah had a strange way of pursing her lips when she was ANGRY.

To My Lovely Wife

On Our 43rd Anniversary, May 19, 2016

I can't believe it's been forty three years
Since we both said "I do"
But here we are my dear
You're still with me and I with you

It seems as it were only yesterday
When down the aisle
We nervously made our way
And I stood before your beautiful smile

It was then our wonderful journey began
Our bags were packed and we were set
So young and eager, we almost ran
To board the waiting Whisper Jet

Like the jet, time has flown
The journey thus far has been great
In wisdom and love, we've both grown
For the next forty three, I can hardly wait

"CAN'T WE PUT THESE PROBLEMS TO HUMAN"?

The Golfer's Prayer

Ron Harvey 11/2/1993

The Pro is my Shepherd, I shall not hook or slice
He maketh my ball lie down in green fairways
He leads me around still water hazards
He restoreth my swing
He leads me on cartpaths of asphalt
for his fairway's sake

Yea though I walk the valley of the shadow of triple bogey
I fear no hole
For he art with me
My driver and my putter, they comfort me

He preparest a video tape before me
In the presence of my fellow hackers
He annoints my head with helpful tips
My golf bag overflows

Surely birdies and eagles shall follow me
All the days of my golfing life
And I shall dwell in the clubhouse of the Pro forever

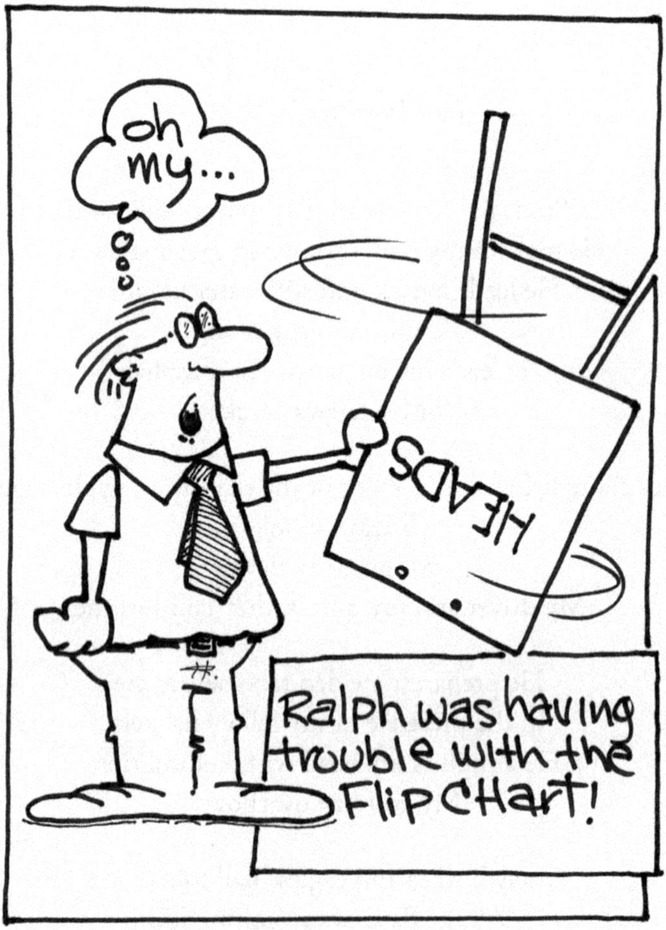
oh my...
HEADS
Ralph was having trouble with the FlipCHart!

Great Expectorations

Ron Harvey

Greetings and salivations! Cuspidor collectors congregate! Spittoon Splatterers unite! Ex members of SA (Spitters Anonymous) are welcome as well. Join me for a brief look at some great moments in spitting history and some do's and don'ts for the modern expectorator. It's quite easy to imagine how spitting first became popular if one transports himself to the first fireside meals of the then not modern cavemen. "Ugh -patooie", haaaaaack, toooie, uunnng hock, phhhhhhhthunk, This loosely translates into "Ugh patooie! Wooly mammoth still a bit wooly, need to stay in fire longer!"

Can you imagine the bits of grit and other undesireable inclusions and intrusions into a caveman's carry out meal that required some very serious expurgation?

Fortunately, spitting has evolved into the fine art it is today. All one has to do is watch a major league baseball game to witness some major league "spitulations",

Spitting actually underwent an evolutionary revolutionary period (known as the ERP era) during the days of the Wild West. Most of the poor spitters either chocked to death or were shot by the more refined spitters. Therefore, the gene pool was gradually narrowed down by "survival of the Spittest",

To further ensure the further evolution of spitters, here are a few rules to follow:

1. Never try to spit out of an airplane window
2. Never chew tobacco on a first date, unless she asks you to try her brand
3. Never spit in someone's face when it 40 degrees below.
4. It's okay to spit in a Dentist's office
5. Never let children between the ages of two and five see you spit. Their Mother's will have a strong dislike for you.
6. Always have a good reason to spit: i.e., a bad tasting oyster, you feel something crawling on your tongue, or you have a mouthful of something you just cant swallow
7. Never try to spit between the gap in your front teeth, especially if you don't have one
8. Never try to spit while while regurgitating. Immediately before or after is okay
9. Never pass gas in bed, then spit into the air causing the wife to immediately jerk the sheets over her head.

THE PODIATRIST COWBOY LIKED HIS BONE SPURS.

Collard Greens

(A dear friend and old golfing buddy of mine always planted a garden and gave generously from it. He was also a Master Woodworker and GAVE me a beautiful oak hall table, a rocking chair, and an oak water bucket. As yet, I haven't written about those, but maybe I will. I miss my old friend - Claude Connell (1935 -2010).

Them shore was some mighty good greens
I et them with taters, chicken and beans
one helping just wasn't quite enough
so some more in my belly I did stuff

When I shoved my legs under the table
to eat the whole pot, I thought I was able
I coulda' et and et, and et a few more
but I woulda' got stuck in the kitchen door

Now dingy dangy alas and alack
I can't seem to push my chair back
A chillin' thought I just seen
I hope there ain't no streaks of green!

What a frightnin' and chillin' thought
Racing to the bathroom all distraught
Thankful I didn't have onions and leeks
Or surely there'd be, smelly green streaks

EVERYONE KNEW CHARLES WOULD SPEARHEAD THE PROJECT.

How Halloween Happened

by
Ron Harvey
Copyright ©November 1, 1993

Goblins, ghouls, ghosts, and gremlins
They're enough to start you a'tremblin
The cauldron's a'bubblin and a'brewin
What's that old witch got a'stewin?

Vampires, zombies, mummies, and black cats
Membranous winged mammals, known as bats
Yellow and orange, triangular eyed pumpkin
Things in the night that go a'bumpkin

Halloween, Halloween, scare me some more
blood, guts, gristle and gore
Graveyards, tombstones, and the living dead
Cause me to hide under my bed

Whooooo started this eerie ritual of October? I believe it began in the village of Sleepy Holler, the home of screaming narcoleptics. There was a rather gruesome looking individual who worked in the local butcher's shop. Every evening after work, he took a dozen or so wieners home for dinner. This wasn't so strange, but it was the manner in which he carried them home that was. Since the hermetically sealed dinner pack was yet to be invented, he carried the wieners home in a large German beer mug. Soon, the local villagers were calling him "Franks in Stein". One day (October 31, 1666) while Franks in Stein was walking home, he was unmugged and robbed of his wieners. Not to be taken lightly, Franks in Stein devised a plan. The next day he filled his large German beer mug with fake wieners. When the "unmuggers" stopped him this time, he tricked them with a treat of "hollow wieners". Franks in Stein really loved wieners - almost to the point of worshiping them. The local folk began calling them his "hallowed wieners". After Franks in Stein died, they began a tradition in his honor. Every October 31st they would dress up in butchers garb and fill large German beer mugs with a mixture of hollow wieners and real wieners. They called it Hallowed Wiener night and walked around town offering wiener "tricks" or "treats" to hapless visiting tourists. This may account for the reason that Sleepy Holler never had a booming tourist trade. After the tourists stopped coming to Sleepy Holler, the villagers began pulling this stunt from door to door.

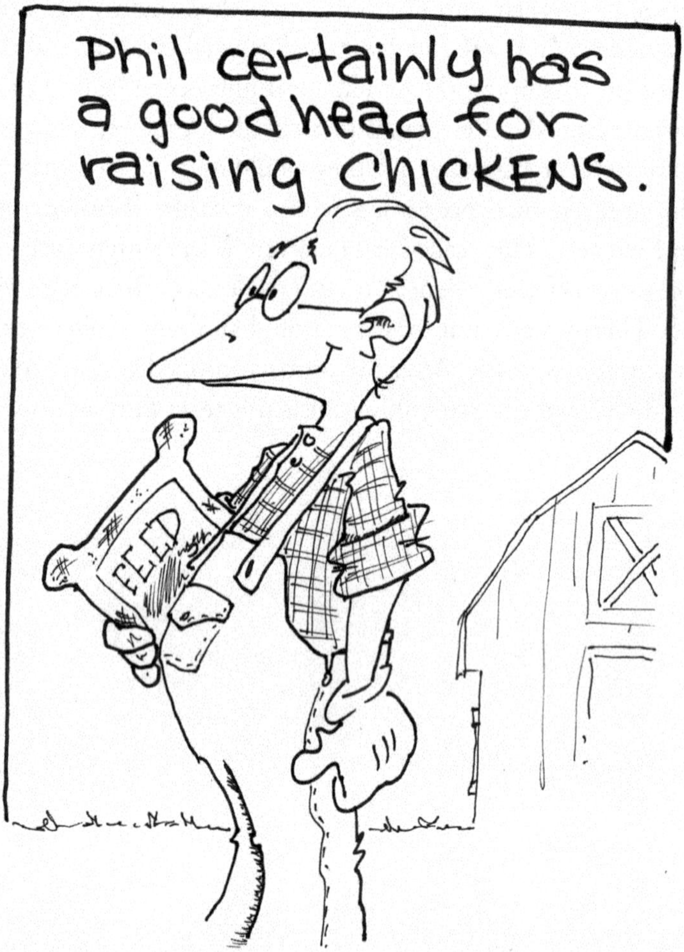
Phil certainly has a good head for raising CHICKENS.
FEED

Happy Birthday to My Wife

This is dedicated to the one i love

Without you, my life would be mt
For me, you were meant 2b
It's all clear to me now ic
I just hope it's there for u2c

So on this your birthday number 65
I hope you are feeling vibrant and alive
Cause if you ain't, my heart would take a nosedive

I appreciate all that you do
That makes me one of the lucky few
Happy birthday!!

Bob was sentenced to life in PRISM because of his colored past.

Hectot the Ant

There was an ant named hector
who was quite the builder and erector
he could often be found
piling dirt upon his mound
and constantly adding another sector

Ida, the reigning queen
liking what she had seen
invited Hector to dance
and pismired off the other ants
causing quite a stir and scene

The entire mound was abuzz
about Hector their cuz
How could he take a chance
with Ida, the Queen of ants
Hector the Erector was a defector

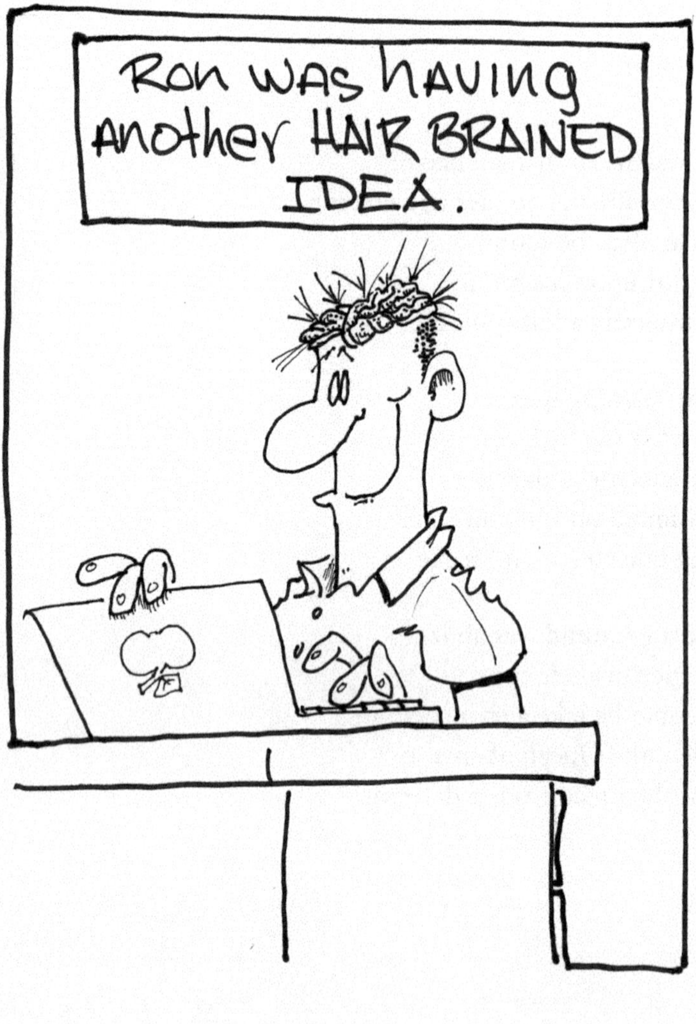
Ron was having another HAIR BRAINED IDEA.

Jockeying for Position

by
Ron Harvey
Copyright © 10/24/93

Did you ever wonder how or why jockey shorts are so named? After going through several drawers of data, I think I've found the answer. During the middle ages, a young french fashion designer by the name of Jacques decided that pantaloons were just too hot and stuffy. Out of shear frustration (scissors weren't invented until the Golden Age), he did a little pantaloons leg lopping. This new fashion was called "Jacques shorts".

Are jockey shorts really worn only by horse jockeys or disc jockeys or is this pure horse hockey? When jockeys wear them are they called jockey jockey shorts? If hockey players wear jockey shorts are they called hockey jockey shorts? What about boxer shorts? If boxers wore jockeys and jockeys wore boxers, would they be called boxer jockey shorts and jockey boxer shorts. Horse jockeys probably invented the phrase, "these shorts are riding up on me"! Boxers actually wear a device called a "cup". Who does the dishes after a bout? I'm not about to. Speaking of dishes, I remember when pretty girls were called "dishes". So, what sort of underwear do "dishes" wear? Panties, of course. With my curiosity "peeked", I went back to the drawers for some more research. Panties were so named due to the rapid breathing young men experienced when they saw women dressed (or undressed) in only their underwear. This rapid breathing condition was known as "the panties".

How about the jock strap? This will be brief. Think about it.... STRAP is PARTS spelled backwards.

Bikini underwear might be more appropriately named "peekini" underwear.

Have you ever wondered why the opening in the front of mens pants and underwear is called the fly?????????

He's been Ballheaded for some time.

Light Humor

by
Ron Harvey
Copyright © 10/24/93

Think about it. Why are lights called lights? Because they're not heavy? I think not. But then again, have you ever left a light burning? In the winter we say, "lets light a fire". That's exactly what we'd have if we left a light burning. A light afire. Why do we say, "turn out the lights"? Have you ever actually "turned" a light to extinguish it? Maybe if it was one that was left burning. That would be a switch.

If lights could fly, could they light on a limb and be alit? Only if they were lightning bulbs.

Whose bright idea was all of this? My guess is that it dates back to medieval times when candles were quite the vogue. Evidently there was a big debate (this was a big contest to see who could remove worms from fishhooks the fastest, but had absolutely nothing to do with candles) as to whether candles should be named candles or cantdles. It was decided that a jousting match (used for lighting jousts) would be held to decide which name should be given to these wicked and waxed illumination devises. Luminaries gathered from afar to witness the event. It was the Duke of Watt versus the Lord of Lumen. The crowd chanted, "kill a watt, kill a watt". The loser lost and the winner won which left the loser "t"eed off, so the "t" was dropped from cantdle and we were left with the word candle. Another more believable version of the origin of the word candle is that candles were originally sold in cans and were referred to as canned light. This was shortened to canned "L". Oh, to wax philosophical is a wicked thing to do, but not to worry, it's beginning to "taper"......

Thomas Edison had nothing better to do than sit around all day eating peppermints and spearmints. When he had his "fill a mints", he invented the light bulb.

Light fixtures are so called because the first light repairman (a ninety-five pound guy named Bulbba) said after his first service call, "I fixed yer light". I wonder if he used a light socket...wrench?

Baseball also has a light related term - "switchhitters". These were kids who were too short to reach light switches so they used baseball bats to hit them. Not all the time, just...off and on. Of course, their mothers would cut short switches to switch these short wearing short kids shorting switches. Obviously this wasn't short enough, so I'll switch subjects.

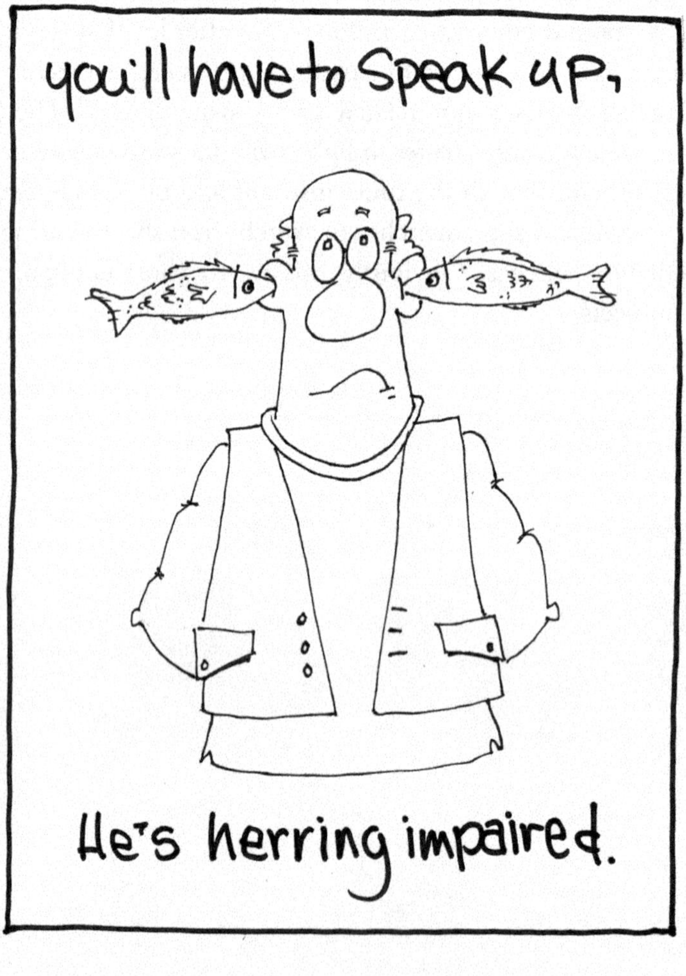
you'll have to Speak up,
He's herring impaired.

The Litterbug

by
Ron Harvey
Copyright © November 2, 1993

I have a theory as to why people litter. The name probably originated from the fact that litter "bugs" most decent and environmentally friendly people. As a matter of fact, bugs have more respect for our environment than people who litter. It almost has to be a genetic defect. Gregor Mendel, the Moravian monk who discovered the principles of inheritance of individual traits in garden peas, could have made an interesting study by crossbreeding litterbugs. But then again, maybe they would have just tossed his studies out of a window. "Sorry Gregor, I'd like to take part in your study but I feel an inherited urge to go to a fast garden pea food chain store and buy a double pea whopper with cheese so I can toss the bag and 30 extra napkins out of my cart window."

I wonder; who was the first litterbug? Could it have been Peking Man after he stopped by one of those oriental fast food places on his way back to Olduvai Gorge? I don't know if I can really blame him if he was the first litterbug. It was probably tough enough to eat fast food, much less keep trash off the pathways while riding atop a mastadon. He probably needed both hands to hold on to the careening behemoth while riding back home to his cave. Since the modern day litterbug has no such excuse, there must be other reasons for such displays of wanton disregard for scenic preservation.

Regardless of who the first litterbug was, he has plenty of dismally decadent descendants hell bent on preserving his trashing tradition.

Could it be there is a secret ingredient or drug present in carry out food and drink? Believe it or not, analysis of food and beverage roadside residue has proven the presence of a foreign substance. It has been identified generically as "ibethrosum" (as in "I be throw some" more trash out the window). Ibethrosum should not be confused with Ibuprofen. Ibuprofen makes headaches go away but ibethrosum gives other people headaches. This secret ingredient probably produces a temporary hypnotic state that causes these otherwise considerate and caring individuals to suffer extreme cases of buyers and eaters remorse. They become so repulsed by the fact they actually purchased and ate everything in the bag or box, they feel compelled to get rid of the evidence. So out the window it goes. I know this to be true of most beer drinkers. They are less resistant to the mesmerizing effects of ibethrosum because the alcohol has an additive effect in combination with ibethrosum. Quite often the effects of ibethrosum are triggered by the sight of a stop sign or the last bite or swallow. Science has yet to find an antidote.

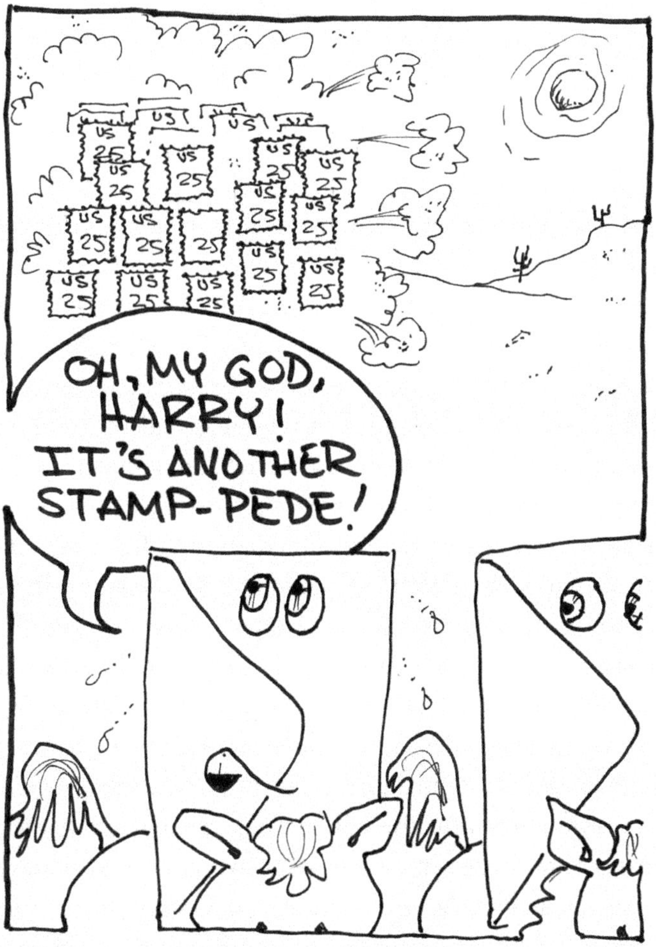
OH, MY GOD, HARRY! IT'S ANOTHER STAMP-PEDE!

Making Sense of Nonsense

Ron Harvey 3/2/2014

What incenses me is incense with no scents. It just doesn't make sense since spending several cents for scents should make sense. This is just pure nonsense for non-scented incense. It's all about the aroma. But just what is a roma? Something doesn't smell right or the entire premise is going up in smoke. Why is incense called incense and where did it originate? If I had to guess, I would speculate that it originally originated in India from burning cow patties as a means of disposal or for keeping warm. Which sensibly brings us back to what is a roma. As you can well imagine, the smoke emanating from the smoldering cow patties would be rather offensive to ones' sense of smell. These malodorous emanations would cause some of the cow patty burners to roam away from the immediate vicinity of the smoldering pile. Those who dutifully remained referred to anyone who left as "a roamer" which through local dialect, was later shortened to a roma. It was actually the romas who invented incense. They came up with the idea to incorporate curry into the cow patties in an attempt to make the smoldering cow patties smell less offensive and no one took offense to this particular defense. But honestly, the curry didn't quite cut it, so the romas began experimenting with other ingredients such as lilac and lavender. Lo and behold, it actually worked and everyone was able to sit around the smoldering cow patties and enjoy the warmth and wafting smoke. The romas were so pleased with their idea that they began charging several rupees for the ingredients. The others became incensed at the idea of being charged so many cents to eliminate the bad scents, which made good sense. In retaliation, they charged at the romas to retaliate before it was too late. This incensed the romas, which is why odors are called aromas and incense is called incense which should all make sense.

Clothes Friends and Close Calls

by
Ron Harvey
Copyright © 6/12/93 - Revised 7-1-93

Once, a Pun of Thyme, and a man named Noah moved from the tiny town of Thyme just in time. You see, the Ewe Sea was near Bye, which is another town a short time from Thyme. Justin, the Nick of Thyme, was a clothes friend of Noah before everyone knew Noah as Noah. Through a Quirk of Fate (there were many quirks in the town of Fate, as fate would have it) Noah's name was changed from NaOH because of a bad reaction. Needless to say (there were no needles in Volved, which just happens to be the town where this incident occurred) there were many caustic remarks to B. Herd. Mr. B. Herd was to blame but let's leave it be. Some things were just not mint to B. Herd, but perhaps another herb instead.

Back to Justin, the Nick of Thyme. Justin was always flipping knickels with his knuckles. One day, a not so sharp shooter of arrows of the cross bow crossed Beaux (the river between Bye and Thyme) and saw Justin beneath the bridge knuckle flipping knickels. Well, it just so happened that the not so sharp shooter was amiss. A miss who couldn't resist taking a shot at one of the flipping knickles. Smiling, as she drew back the bow, she put away the pencil and paper and let the arrow fly (an arrow fly is a small fly lost in Thyme). I'm sure you've heard that a miss is as good as a smile. In this (brief) case, the smile exerted a slight excess of pressure on her right eye muscles and caused her aim to be a bit off target. As for who bit it off, I don't know.

By now (actually bye later, for the story's not finished) you might have guessed, the arrow nicked the nickel and the nickel nicked Nick. Hence, he became the Nick of Thyme. It was a clothes call, after all, because he had to call the clothing store for more clothes. "Help, he said, I've just had an arrow escape and I must say, I need some new clothes." Who Do You Think worked at the clothing store but was out ill that day so Noah worked for him in Stead (the town where the clothing store was located.) Justin was relieved (at this point, an underwear statement) to speak with Noah. It was often said (although not too often, since repeating things was repetitious and difficult in this particular instance) that: "no nose knows clothes like Noah's nose." In this case Noah's nose knew Justin needed new clothes. This is why Justin and Noah were clothes friends.

Looks like the CAPTAIN is entering DATA into his Log again.
DATA

Pairing Perplexities or A Brief Treatise on the Disappearance of Sock Mates

Soon, I shall rename this facility the Ponder-osa since you've begun these incessantly insidious, yet inanely insipid questions, and I find myself pondering pointlessly with a penchant. Exactly from whence the penchant came, I haven't been able to ascertain but I believe it originated with the early lexicographers and their ritualistic chants about pens. This sounds reasonable until you realize that early lexicographers didn't have pens (well, they did but they probably kept pigs in them and you certainly cant write with those). They probably practiced calligraphy with large feathers (probably pin feathers). Whatever this may have to do with the disappearance of socks in the modern day washers and dryers, I have no earthly idea.

Lost sock sightings have been reported from as far away as Stockholm (erstwhile Sockholm or Stockingholm) It has not been totally dis-proven that socks have minds of their own and prefer to travel alone instead of in pairs which accounts for their propensity to exit washers and dryers mateless. The greatest invention I've ever encountered is the Sock Lock. This device was introduced to me by none other than George John. To appreciate the full impact of this introduction, one would need to travel with George. I would recommend for you to continue losing socks. The Sock Lock is a plastic ring with inwardly pointing protrusions to entrap a pair of socks and prevent their unwanted disappearance. Lately however, my sock locks have been disappearing. Could it be that I have "sockabilistic" (derived from cannibalistic) washer or dryer??

I believe sock losing actually began in rural America and is carried on as a tradition by today's sock descendants. Before the advent of Maytag, there was Momtag. She would haul (as well as haul wood) the month's dirties down to the creek for a quick cleansing. The socks saw this as an opportunity to take a little swim (besides, they didn't really like getting scrubbed on those old timey washboards). Unfortunately, many of these socks were unable to swim back upstream either because they were full of holes or overly encrusted with layers of toe jam, and were left to float downstream until they were snagged from their watery demise by some creel crazy trout fisherman who thought he had landed supper.

There are those who believe that this is pure poppycock and that socks are vaporized in the dryer cycle. They believe it is really a Communist plot to destroy our sanity by making us wear mismatched socks to work, It seems that there is also a faction who believe that certain elements of the Communist society infiltrated several silk sock and stocking weaving plants and covertly introduced technologically advanced materials into the sock looms. These materials were either water soluble so they caused the socks to disappear in the washer, or were heat sensitive so the sock would disappear in the dryer.

Who invented socks? Who was the first person to wear socks and what was his or her reaction when he or she put the first one on? Did it have a little fuzzy ball on the heel?

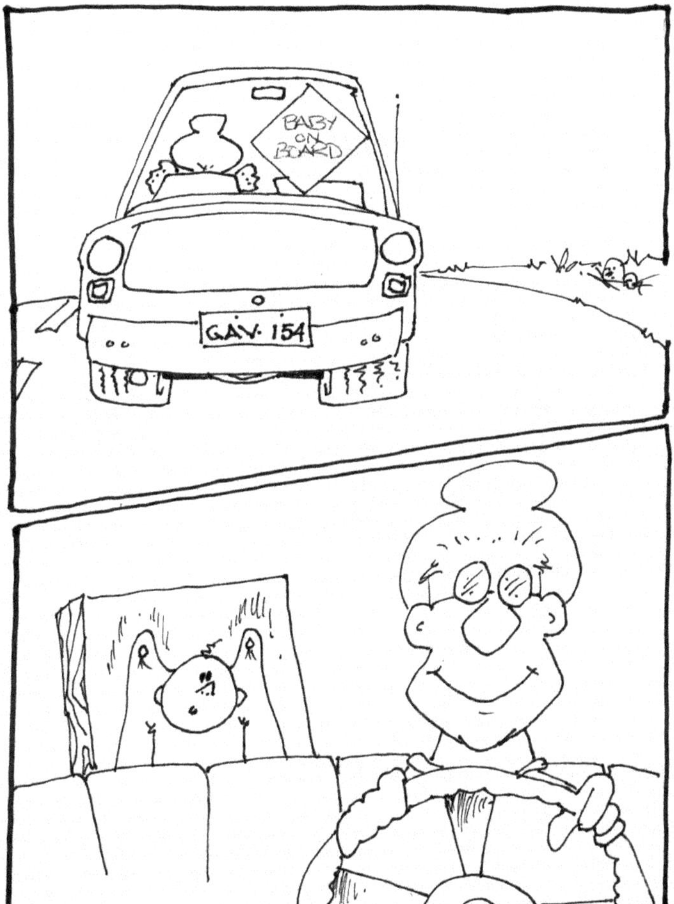
BABY ON BOARD
GAV·154

Parking Lot Partners

By
Ron Harvey

I parked my car next to your car
Now we are parking lot partners, by dingy
Sad to say, but yesterday
I parked too close, by dingy
My door slammed into your door
Now I can't be your your parking lot partner any more
Now you have a nice little scratch
Just about two inches below your latch
I must learn to be more careful
Lest I get an earful
Parking lot partners no more
All because dinged your dang door
Wham, bam, slam, oops I'll be damned
dingy dangy walla walla bing bangy

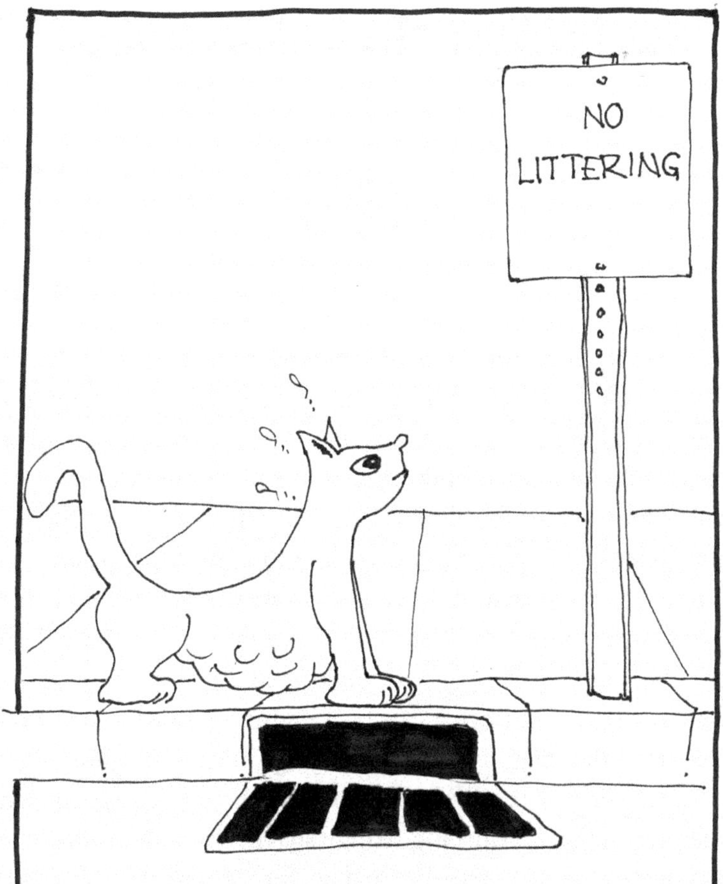
NO
LITTERING

Peanut Butter and Jellyfish Sandwich or "Its A Shore Thing"

By
Ron Harvey
Copyright © November 2000

As Christine told me, Ait=s one of those things that sound right, but it just isn=t. I could not agree with her more. I enjoy a good peanut butter and jelly sandwich every now and then and will occasionally have a fish sandwich. Come to think of it, a peanut butter and jelly AND fish sandwich may not be all that bad. But Christine=s concoction of a peanut butter and jellyfish sandwich, although it may sound good, just doesn=t seem all that appetizing. For one thing, it would require a couple of rather large bread slices just to contain one of those slippery rascals. Just keeping the jelly within the confines of the bread in a Anormal@ PB & J sandwich can be a daunting task in and of itself. Can you imagine tangling with tenacious tentacles dangling over the crusts edge? Perhaps the PB& JF sandwich would be best consumed in a manner similar to slurping stringy spaghetti.

Another thought just occurred to me: if you were desperately hungry enough to actually eat a PB & JF sandwich, where would you obtain a jellyfish in the first place? I am not sure if they would be readily available at the local deli, so the best bet would be the local beach. They wash ashore in abundance and with relative frequency so you should have no problems finding one suitable for sandwiching. Once you have selected the right one, it must be thoroughly washed to remove all of the beach sand. If not, you will end up with a peanut butter and jellyfish sand sandwich which is a mouthful.

I wonder if there are grape jellyfish or strawberry jellyfish? I=ll bet orange marmalmermaid jellyfish would be good with peanut butter. The dilemma in making such a preposterous but Aright sounding@ sandwich is the choice of peanut butter. Which brand would be best? Jiffy, Skippy, or Peter Pan? Crunchy or smooth? People may accuse you of being a little Askippy@ if you were to make a PB & JF sandwich in the first place. Peter Pan is definitely out of the question unless you believe in jellyfish fairy tales. That leaves crunchy Jiffy which makes perfect sense. You would certainly want to finish eating in a jiffy, and crunchy because it would make you realize you were nuts.

The Feat of The Effete Feet Defeat of Pete LaFite's Feet

Copyright © 1993 by Ron Harvey

The feet of Pete LaFite were two feet measuring two feet per foot. The feat of the defeat of his two feet feet is truly an amazing story.

LaFite's famous feet fought in ferocious foot fights frequently. Challengers would foot fight tooth and toenail but none could gain the upper foot on LaFite. During these foot fights, his feet flailed flawlessly and never failed. His feet were undefeated and not the least bit effete. Once Pete's feet got a toe hold on his opponent, the match was over. After the match, Pete would treat himself and his opponent to a foot massage, and Pete would foot the bill and say, "I toed you so."

In spite of Pete's famous feet, they presented podiatrical problems. No matter where Pete went, he made a big impression. Pete LaFite's feet were so large that when he walked barefoot through the mud, the mudsucking sounds frightened farm animals and caused small children to hide under beds. The odor from Pete LaFite's feet once caused a squeamish shoe salesman to have fits of nausea and finally faint. The store manager had to blow a shoe horn to revive him. It's true that Pete had a problem too big for DeseneXXXX.

Pete's personal podiatrist pondered Pete's problem from a safe distance. "Eureka!", he exclaimed. Pete replied, "I know that, so what are you going to do about it?" The puzzled podiatrist devised a plan to trick Pete into wearing shoes, socks, and odor eaters. He would bring in a "ringer" to foot fight LaFite. The loser would have to cover his prized feet with shoes and socks. Everyone was Scholl on the idea.

Short Stories to Amuse, Baffle, and Educate

The "ringer", with effete petite feet, arrived with bells on and chimed, "I'm here to defeat Pete LaFite's two too famous two feet feet." Pete accepted the challenge and the foot fight began. The ringer called Pete a big heel and socked him. After the ringer had the socks on Pete's feet, Pete couldn't get a toe hold on his opponent's petite feet and was finally defeated. You might say the ringer approached this foot fight "from a different ankle." This made Pete hopping mad so he grabbed his left foot in his left hand and left town by hopping along Cassidy Street and then hippity hopping down the Bunion Trail. The spectators followed and soon got on the right track. Pete LaFite was brought back fit to be tied and was tied and fit with what appeared to be a pair of "lace up" shoes.

One would think there would be a moral to this story, but there isn't.

Note on the Two Politol letters:

These should be dedicated to H. T. DelliColli, Phd., (1944 ------) a brilliant and reknown Surface Chemist. He wrote Politol 1 to me as a jokingly legitimate letter (obviously, I had to "officially "respond). He was a colleague and former Manager of mine when I worked in our Agrichenicals lab. We formulated herbicides based on tree derived dispersants and surfactants which were sold to AG Chem companies worldwide.

Short Stories to Amuse, Baffle, and Educate

RECEIVED JUN 1 9 1995

Muldoon Industries Inc.
7B-13 Sweeney Industrial Park
Oiledbutt, AR 72702

Mr. Ronald K. Harvey
Manager of Fats and Oils
Westvaco Inc.
P. O. Box 70848
Charleston, SC 29415-0848

Dear Mr. Harvey:

A friend of mine in the rendering business has given me your name and suggested that I contact you for assistance.

Muldoon Industries is a small rendering operation which processes offal from several local slaughterhouses which supply the pet food industry with meat.

We produce several grades of tallow which are sold to the soap industry. One of our most profitable products, MUL-EFA-T®, is made from the scraps we receive from a mule processing plant in Little Rock. This product is a very pale yellow material which has carried a premium price. However, Muldoon Industries has recently entered into an agreement with the states of Arkansas, Tennessee, and Missouri to process road kill. The tallow from this operation is blended with the MUL-EFA-T to produce the raw material for a highly priced complexion soap sold on the local economy.

Our problem is this; in the spring, the road kill from Missouri and Arkansas contains a high percentage of opossum fragments. These cause the tallow to have a very dark amber color. This, in turn, causes the soap manufacturer to have to bleach the material before he uses it.

Do you have a product similar to POLITOL NA which we can use to remove the color bodies from opossum fat?

Also, we will begin taking yellow grease from a large chain of fast food restaurants in the southeast. This particular chain specializes in deep fried small game. Once again, the dark color of opossum fat further tainted with traces of raccoon and armadillo fat pose a problem. Can you help us here?

Please call me at our toll free number 800-845-1983 to discuss the possibility of some laboratory and plant trials.

Very truly yours,

K. Skritch
Manager of Operations

cc: Edward Muldoon
President and CEO

Ron Harvey

Westvāco

June 20, 1995

BCC: H. T. DelliColli
L. S. Eppersimons
A. S. Hill
B. G. Marsi
T. F. McPartland
E. A. Rose
C. A. Squier
C.   Symmes

Mr. K. Skritch
Muldoon Industries Inc.
7B-13 Sweeney Industrial Park
Oiledbutt, AR 72702

Dear Mr. Skritch:

Thank you for your interest in our products. POLITOL® has been utilized in a vast array of rendering applications. Although POLITOL has never been used in automotively masticated animal viscera, I, in my matutinal mentations, can think of no reason why POLITOL® DOA will not work.

POLITOL® DOA is a newly developed product designed and tested by our brilliant technical staff. They have spent countless hours scraping road kill for testing and are offally deadicated to product improvement. Once, they became so engrossed in their work, they failed to see an approaching semi and are now working a little shorthanded. One of them is a little short legged, but this seems to aid in retrieving road kill from steep embankments.

Opossum fat poses an unusual problem in most reclamation facilities. The most effective way to use POLITOL® DOA, as recommended by our technical staff, is through digital manipulation into the anal aperture (of the opossum, armadillo, or raccoon) prior to the rendering operation. Make sure the animal is dead first or you could receive a nasty bite. Dosages will vary depending upon elapsed time since impact and the amount of opossum still intact.

Thank you again for your interest. If I can be of further assistance, please call me at 1-800-OIL-DROP.

Still Warm Regards,

R. K. Hahvey,
Manager of Fats & Oils (MOFO)

cc: Edward Muldoon
      President and CEO

Chemical Division
Box 70848
Charleston Heights, SC 29415-0848
Telephone 803 740 2300

A Poodle Piddling Poem

by Ron Harvey
Copyright ©11/13/92
Dedicated to The Memory of Sharon K. Hicks

Have you ever paddled a poodle because
it piddled in a puddle?

A pool of poodle piddle is preposterous
'pecially if it makes you mutter muttily

Poodles piddle prolifically, or so it seems
with a piddle puddle here, and a piddle puddle there

EEEE IIII EEEE IIII OH, I yell
please please puppy poodle

this piddling has to stop
now, where the heck is the mop?????

> BLAKE couldn't remember where he left his glasses — or we're not sure if they were half full or empty.

Residential Residents and Presidential Presidents

Ron Harvey
4/22/2016

This is dedicated to young Mr. Stephen Jones. I had given a copy to his father (Dr. Steve Jones) to give to Stephen. While sitting in church one Sunday, Steve discovered this in his coat pocket and gave it to Stephen. He said that as Stephen read it, he began laughing and couldn't stop.

While it is true that residential residents reside in residences and Presidential Presidents reside and preside in Presidential and residential residences, it is not necessarily true that there is such a thing as a hackle shackle tackle debacle. One might logically ask, "how in the world are these two things possibly related?" The answer is simple: they are not. I suppose I could contrive a perfectly illogical logical relationship totally non-relative to any of my relatives (except for one), but I would prefer to relate that later when it is more relative to my relatives. I do have relatives residing in residential residences however, I have no relatives residing in Presidential residential residences. This sequence of non-sequined sequences (can sequences even be sequenced with sequins?). I suppose if they could, that would be an odd coincidence consequence which brings me to the Theory of Relativity:

Aren't we all related? If Adam and Eve were the first two humans, then everyone on earth is related, which is relatively relative as well as revealing (revealing is when you have a second helping of veal which reveals that you have real zeal for veal). Veal can do that. It is known as veal appeal or the real veal deal. When the USDA puts their Red Dye #2 stamp on it, it is the Real Veal Deal Seal. You do realize that veal doesn't come from a seal. Those are aquatic mammals which are totally irrelevant and occasionally irreverent. Their fate has been sealed as has mine....

Orthoptera Blattidae or La Cucaracha

*by Ron Harvey
Copyright © 1993*

Perhaps you don't recognize the order and family of this well known pest. Okay, one more hint. Genus and species, Periplaneta americana. I think it translates; all over the planet and america. I can think of no useful function it serves other than to keep pest control companies in business. It's the American cockroach. As if one genus and species isn't enough, we are also blessed with the brown-banded, Oriental, and German cockroaches. Would you believe there are more than 2,000 recorded species in the world?

These adept scurriers didn't just fall off the garbage truck yesterday. They've been around since the Carboniferous age, a mere 200,000,000 years ago. I guess it's better they survived rather than the dinosaurs. A Tyrannosaurus Rex would have been a little more difficult to stomp. It certainly would have required a bigger shoe. Of course, they wouldn't be quite the scurriers and would have probably required a much costlier amount of pesticide. But, look on the bright side: they couldn't hide under the kitchen cabinets as easily. Everthing's a trade-off.

I could never figure out if the song, "La Cucaracha" was about someone trying to get out of the way of one of these "super 'sects" or trying to run one down to apply a stomp. Whatever the case, it's a lively and spirited song and dance. Most people, especially women, do both simultaneously. That is, try to apply a stomp and get out of the way at the same time while emitting ear piercing shrieks of hysteria.

They make such lovely sounds when a stomp is properly applied. If properly executed, the roach stomp should produce a resounding pop. To achieve the ultimate "pop", coax the roach onto a wooden floor.

Linoleum will suffice. This will also cause most women to break into their versions of "La Cucaracha" and emit ear piercing shrieks of hysteria. Quite often they will utter sounds of disgust as well.

Did you ever notice that when they die, they don't really die? They always have a leg or two that just won't give up. Just kill one and toss it into the old thunder bowl. Before you can reach the flush lever, he'll be doing the roach paddle trying to reach the porcelain shore line. Why is it that when they've been poisoned, they go to the middle of a room (especially when quests are present), turn over onto their backs and do leg lifts? I think it's a defiant and obscene gesture on their part.

I don't believe it was a serpent that tricked Eve into eating that apple, but another of those 2,000 species of roaches. Noah didn't have to go out and round up two for his forty day cruise either. They probably just followed his trail of unleavened bread crumbs right onto the ark. He should have refused them boarding passes.

— Leif Erikson —.
NORSE EXPLORER
Father of CAMOFLAGE

Ron Harvey

June 20, 1995
Mr. K. Skritch
Muldoon Industries Inc.
7B-13 Sweeney Industrial Park
Oiledbutt, AR 72702

Dear Mr. Skritch:

Thank you for your interest in our products. POLITOL7 has been utilized in a vast array of rendering applications. Although POLITOL has never been used in automotively masticated animal viscera, I, in my matutinal mentations, can think of no reason why POLITOL7 DOA will not work.

POLITOL7 DOA is a newly developed product designed and tested by our brilliant technical staff. They have spent countless hours scraping road kill for testing and are offally deadicated to product improvement. Once, they became so engrossed in their work, they failed to see an approaching semi and are now working a little shorthanded. One of them is a little short legged, but this seems to aid in retrieving road kill from steep embankments.

Opossum fat poses an unusual problem in most reclamation facilities. The most effective way to use POLITOL7 DOA, as recommended by our technical staff, is through digital manipulation into the anal aperture (of the opossum, armadillo, or raccoon) prior to the rendering operation. Make sure the animal is dead first or you could receive a nasty bite. Dosages will vary depending upon elapsed time since impact and the amount of opossum still intact.

Thank you again for your interest. If I can be of further assistance, please call me at 1-800-OIL-DROP.

> Still Warm Regards,
> R. K. Hahvey,
> Manager of Fats & Oils (MOFO)
> cc: Edward Muldoon
> President and CEO

Ron's Sick Get Well Card

Just a little get well note
From an crusty old goat
To let you know
I been think'n bout yo

I shoulda bought a card
I coulda bought a card
But my butt has too much lard
So I'll try instead to be a bard

And send my wishes
To someone delicious
To feel better soon
And go howl at the moon

You've always been a giver
Now you have a little less liver
The mere thought makes me shiver
Now we'll call you Ms de-liver

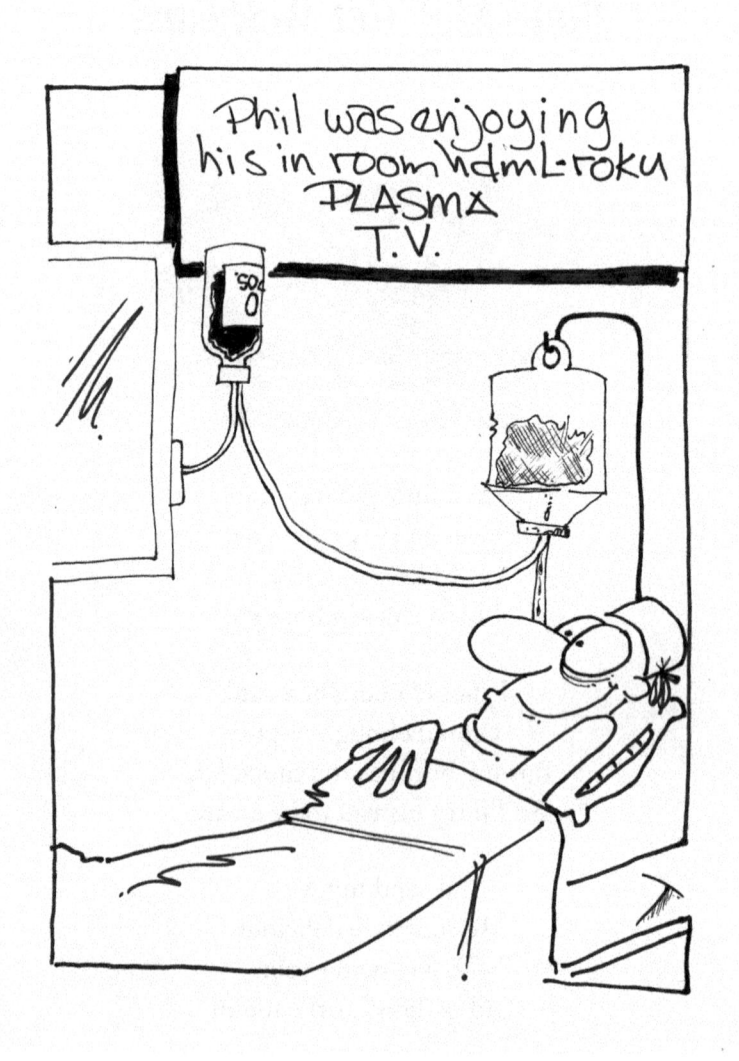

Phil was enjoying his in room hdmI-roku PLASMA T.V.

The Naming of The Shoe

by
Ron Harvey
Copyright © October 17, 1993

Perhaps it all began as a result of early man stepping on dirt clods. Over the years, these clods hardened as a result of non-glacier action and mans' foot didn't. Hence they began hopping over the hardened clods and promptly became known as clod-hoppers. Occasionally, one of these clod-hopping clod hoppers would misjudge the distance and not quite clear the clod causing grievous injury to the bottom rear of his foot. Due to the location of the injury, it required several weeks to heal. It is my understanding that this is why the heel is called a heel. After decades of abortive attempts at clod-hopping and subsequent heel healing, hardened scar tissue formed on that portion of the foot because of the repetitive "heelings." It's a callous thing to say, but this is what inspired Barry Manilow to write his song, "Feelings", which was originally titled "Heelings."

Legend also has it that the lively and spirited dance known as clogging was invented by the short jumping clod-hoppers. Since they couldn't jump quite as far as the heelers, chunks of clods would become clogged between their toes (these clogged clod chunks were called clogs) and the lively and spirited dances were invented to dislodge the clogs. Necessity was not the mother of invention, clogs were. If the dancing was not enough to dislodge the clods, they would shower their feet with gourds of water. The dislodged clogs were called "shower clogs."

These long and short jumping clodhoppers were from a nomadic tribe known as the Archies because of the way they arched themselves over the larger clods. Those tribal members unable to remain standing after a clod arching episode were called fallen Archies.

So, how does the shoe fit in all of this? With the advent of the glacier age, the clods disappeared - which was an ice thing to happen. The Archies missed their clod hopping, heel healing, clog dislodging days so they began having clod hopping contests to commemorate their days of yore and mine (they were also miners of ore). Tickets were sold for feet around. Contestants and spectators alike ingeniously clad their feet in an assortment of wrappings (known as clad wrap) to protect them during the contests and to give them advantages over their competitors and fellow spectators. Some wrapped their feet in lambs wool so they could sneak in without purchasing a ticket. This type of footwear became known as sneakers. Others used the ends of bird wings because they thought it would help them fly over the big clods. Obviously these were called wing tips. Non-participants who did nothing to help and just generally milled around in footwear that wasn't laced to their feet were known as loafers. Contestants who wore open type footwear that allowed sand to get all over their feet called their footwear "sand alls."

Sheet Suckers

by
Ron Harvey
Copyright August 1993

Having gone to bed some 16,880 times in my life, I've had several opportunities to share sleeping quarters with a variety of snorers. Lest I be misunderstood, they weren't all of the opposite sex. Lest I be further misunderstood, none were in the same bed with the same sex, except for growing up with my brothers. We slept together out of necessity. There were four of us and only two beds, which came in handy on cold nights since the only heat we had was in the front of the house. I'm sure you've heard of how ancient shepherds described how cold a night was by referring to it as a "two dog night" or a "three dog night" depending upon how many English Sheep dogs they had to sleep with to stay warm. We referred to them as "two brother nights" or "three brother nights". I can recall having only one three dog night in my life. I think I picked them up in a bar somewhere around closing time.

Snorers come in all heights, weights, shapes, and nostril sizes. I can only surmise that the larger the nasal opening, the more powerful the snore. Small nasal openings tend to produce higher pitched, ear piercing snores. Actual nasal opening measurements on actively snoring sleepers support this theory. The word "snore" is actually an acronym: Sleeping Nasal Openings Reverberating Eerily.

Lung capacity also plays an important role in producing the many different snore sounds. The greater the amount of air one can inhale through the nostrils, the greater the tendency of the lower outer portion of the nose to be sucked toward the septum. This severely constricts the air passage thereby producing the high pitched snores. The uvula (that little apparatus that hangs in the very back of the roof of your mouth) is the mechanism that produces the snore. It does this by reverberating against the larynx, pharynx, tonsils and epiglottis or whatever else it can find. Lord help you if you have an extended uvula.

For taxonomical purposes, I have classified snores in the following categories:

> The Lint Puller: This snore is one that the bed mate or room sharer can sleep with. The suction created by this pony league snore is merely enough to clear the immediate area of loose lint. The problem with the lint puller is that once the snorer's nose become full of lint he (or she) will start breathing through the mouth. This will lead to:

> The Roof Rattler: Although it doesn't rattle the roof of the house, it rattles around in the roof of the snorer's mouth. The uvula plays a major role. It will also rattle your nerves as well as your brain. Coaxing the person to roll over on his side doesn't help. All this does is create death traps for small bedside insects. Once an insect is inhaled, all sorts of coughing, hacking, and spitting will ensue. Unless, of course, the snorer was dreaming about food.

> The Air Brake Snore: During this snore, not much sound is made during the intake phase. It is during the exhalation phase that this snore gets it's name. It sounds like the air brakes of a large semi being applied at the last minute.

> The Wheeze Whistle: This snore involves the tongue. During most snores the tongue remains inactive, but

not this one. It becomes compressed slightly on the roof of the mouth. Depending on the amount of compression, either a wheeze or a whistle is produced.

The Sheet Sucker: This is the most alarming and frightening snore I've ever witnessed. It is so powerful, that I've had to pull portions of sheets from the nostrils of sleeping victims. Neither lint nor insect will survive. If you know someone who fits this category, I highly recommend that they don't sleep on silk sheets. They are lighter than cotton and much more susceptible to nasal penetration. Silk sheets are also smoother and tend to get sucked farther up the nose. However, they are easier to remove.

All of these snores are divided into three classes: Steady, Intermittent, and Good God Almighty. I don't know which is worse. The Intermittent Wheeze Whistle or The Good God Almighty Air Brake. The Sheet Sucker is in a class all by itself.

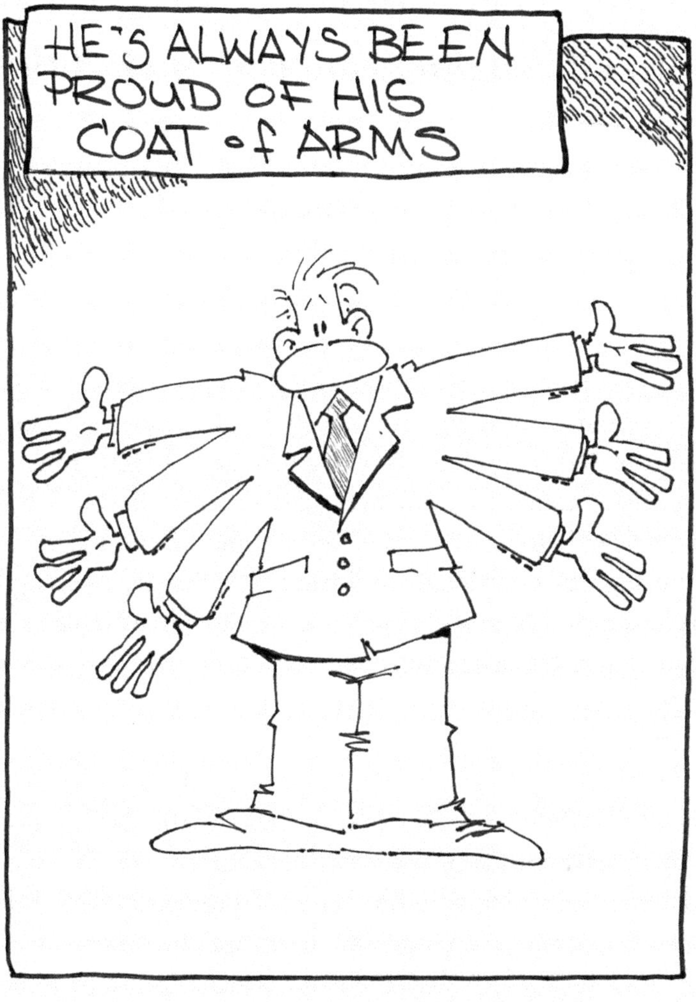
HE'S ALWAYS BEEN PROUD OF HIS COAT of ARMS

Pairing Perplexities or "A Brief Treatise on The Disappearance of Sock Mates"

by
Ron Harvey
Copyright 10/04/1994

Soon, I shall rename this facility "The Ponderosa" since you've begun these incessantly insidious, yet inanely insipid questions, and I find myself "pondering" pointlessly with a penchant. Exactly from whence the penchant came, I haven't been able to ascertain, but I believe it originated with the early lexicographers and their ritualistic chants about pens. This sounds o.k. until you realize that early lexicographers didn't have pens but probably practiced calligraphy with large feathers (probably pin feathers). Whatever this may have to do with the disappearance of socks in the modern day washers and dryers, I have no earthly idea.

Lost sock sightings have been reported as far away as Stockholm (erstwhile Sockholm or Stockingholm). It has not been totally disproved that socks have minds of their own and merely like to travel alone instead of pairs which accounts for their propensity to exit washers and dryers mateless. The greatest invention I've ever encountered is the "sock-lock". This device was introduced to me by none other than George John. To appreciate the full impact of this introduction, one would have to travel with George. I would recommend for you to continue losing socks....... The "sock-lock" is a plastic ring with inwardly pointing protrusions to entrap a pair of socks and prevent their unwanted disappearance. Lately, however, my sock locks have been disappearing. Could it be that I have a "sockabilistic" washer or dryer?

I believe sock losing actually began in rural America and is carried on as a tradition by today's sock descendants. Before the advent of Maytag, there was Momtag. She would haul (as well as haul wood) the months dirties down to the creek for a quick cleansing. The socks saw this as an opportunity to take a little swim (besides, they didn't really like getting scrubbed on those old-timey washboards). Unfortunately, many of these socks were unable to swim back upstream either because they were full of holes or encrusted with layers of toe-jam, and were left to float downstream until they were snagged from their watery demise by some creel crazy trout fisherman who thought he had landed supper.

There are those who believe this is pure poppycock and that socks are really vaporized in the dryer cycle. They believe it is really a communist plot to destroy our sanity by making us wear mismatched socks to work. It seems that there is a faction who believe that certain elements of the communist society infiltrated several silk sock and stocking weaving plants and covertly introduced technologically advanced materials into the sock looms. These materials were either water soluble so that they caused the sock to disappear in the washer, or were heat sensitive so that the sock would disappear in the dryer.

Who invented socks? Who was the first person to wear socks and what was his (or her) reaction when he or she put the first one on? Was it a knee-high or mid-calf? Did it have a little fuzzy ball on the heel?

Taters

Some people never do anything to help, but are gifted at finding fault with the way others do the work. They are called Comment Taters.

Some people are very bossy and like to tell others what to do, but don't want to soil their own hands. They are called Dick Taters.

Some people are always looking to cause problems. It is too hot or too cold, too sour or too sweet. They are called Agie Taters.

There are those who say they will help, but just never get around to actually doing the promised help. They are called Hezzi Taters.

Some people can put up a front and pretend to be someone they are not. They are called Emma Taters.

Then there are those who love others and are always prepared to stop, lend a helping hand. They bring real sunshine into the lives of others. They are called Sweet Taters.

Not sure that I wrote this. If not, someone out there has a mind as warped as mine but I don't mind if they don't mind

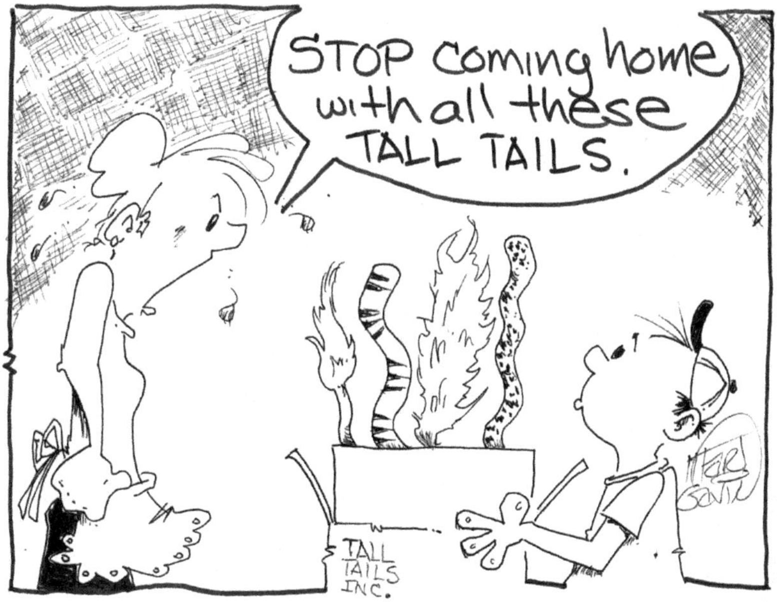
STOP coming home with all these TALL TAILS.
TALL TAILS INC.

The Ant

*By
Ron Harvey
Copyright © 2000*

There once was an ant
who went by the name of Ghant
Given his disposition
was quite prone
to fly into rage and rant.
1Whilst atop his mound
sitting next to a drone
heard the ringing of his cell phone.
Extending his antenna
he fried himself with radiation,
now Ghant is quite gone.

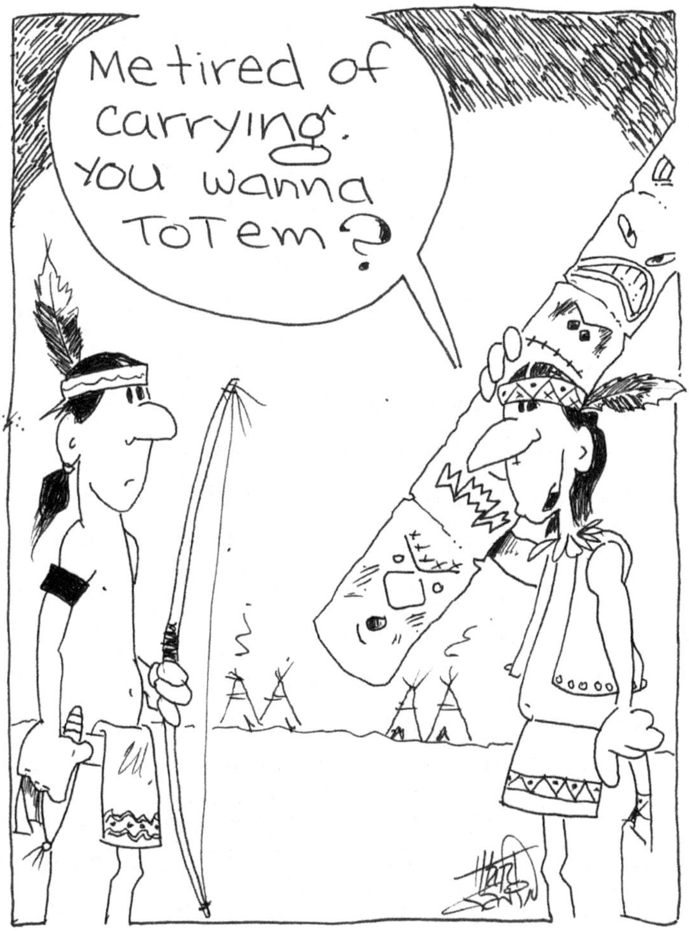
Me tired of carrying. You wanna ToTem?

To My Darling Wife on Our Forty first Anniversary

It seems only yesterday
We were courting and dating
Suddenly now, it is today
And on each other we are still waiting

The things you do for me
Quite often I fail to see
I should appreciate you more
Lest I get knocked to the floor

I don't tell you I love you enough
Probably because my mouth is filled with stuff
It's a poor excuse and I should do better
That is why I'm writing this letter

You are the best a man could have for a wife
Which is why, I will love you for all my life
For the good times and the lean
Both of which we have seen

I will be there at your side
Even when global warming
Raises the tide

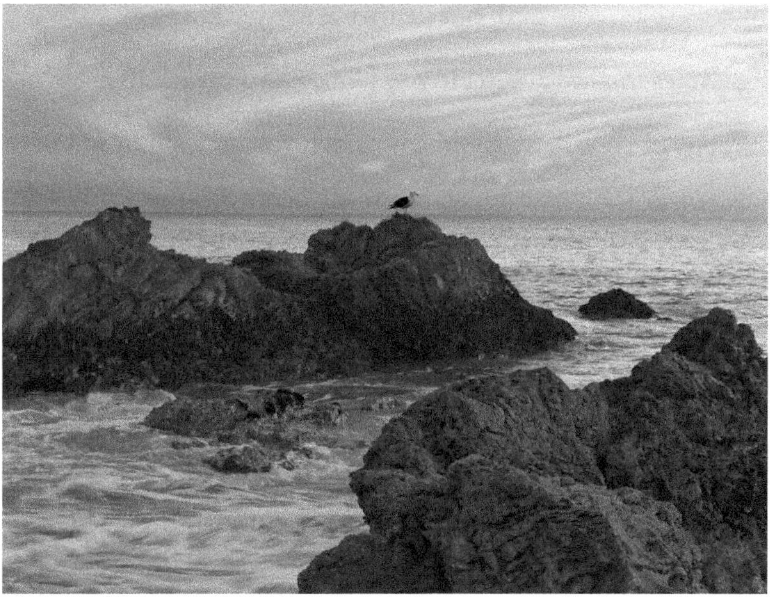

To My Onliest Valentine

Why spend money, when i can make a card for my honey?
It might not be as fancy as a store-bought
card, but neither is my yard.

Roses might have made you faint, and a paramedic i ain't

A box of chocolates could have given you gas, so i took a pass

Jewelry is always nice, but i couldn't afford the price

A new car would have been clutch, but a bit too much

What to give, what to give, oh what to give, tis' the hard part

It was unanimous: all my organs voted and they emoted

"Give her your heart"

How You'se Should Use Yore Yews, Your Yous and Ewes

By
Ron Harvey © February, 2002

First of all, just what is a yore yew? Most people of average intelligence would suspect it should be "your yew" as opposed to yore yew. Think of your days of yore when you could have owned a yew tree. This would have been your yew tree of yore, or if you lived in Pittsburgh, youse yore yew tree. Suppose you (or youse) used your yew tree as a tethering post for your female sheep in those days of your yore. Surely then, your yew of your yore would be for your ewe's use. However, I would imagine, being the highly intellectual person you are, you would chose to use your yews for more profitable ventures than tethering your ewes.

What could possibly be a more profitable use of yews than tethering your yore ewe to your yore yew? Why, hewing your yore yew to make your yo-yos of course. This would leave your yew of yore without a ewe use and you would be a yew yo-yo'er of yore with your new yew yo-yo. People wouldn't call you a yahoo but a yewhoo and when they called for you, it would be: "Yoohoo?? You yewhoo yahoo who hews yews as you'se new yew use - where are you hewing??

Can you imagine the hue and cry had your yore name been Hugh, and Hugh (you) was a yo-yoer of you'se yews you hewed? Heaven forbid should your yew of yore change colors and develop a new yew hue. What on earth would Hugh's hue be? What on earth would Hugh's yew hue be? You who are yew- hewers for your new yew yo-yos or yoohooers for yo-yoer's, take heed (if you can remember where you left it after all of this). Never should you'se use a hued hewed yew yo-yo string to tether your ewe. You'se should use used ewe's yew's cord. And speaking of cord, it's about time to tie a knot in this story.